EX LIBRIS

VINTAGE CLASSICS

ROBERTO BOLAÑO

Roberto Bolaño was born in Santiago, Chile, in 1953. He grew up in Chile and Mexico City, where he was a founder of the Infrarealism poetry movement. Described by the *New York Times* as 'the most significant Latin American literary voice of his generation', he was the author of over twenty works, including *The Savage Detectives*, which received the Herralde Prize and the Rómulo Gallegos Prize when it appeared in 1998, and *2666*, which posthumously won the 2008 National Book Critics Circle Award for Fiction. Bolaño died in Blanes, Spain, at the age of fifty, just as his writing found global recognition.

'For stunning wit, brutal honesty, loving humanity and a
heart that bleeds into the simplest of words,
no other writer ever came close'
Marlon James

'Bolaño's books are volcanic, perilous, charged with infectious
erotic energy and demonic lucidity'
Benjamín Labatut

'An exemplary literary rebel'
New York Review of Books

'Bolaño is the writer who opened a new vein for twenty-first-
century literature . . . Vivacious and weird and madly alive again'
Kevin Barry

'Bolaño's uncontrollable storytelling pulsion, his savage way of
using adjectives, his melancholic, almost tormented urban
realism, changed the tone of a whole tradition'
Álvaro Enrigue

'When I read Bolaño, I think: everything is possible again'
Nicole Krauss

'Bolaño made each book more ambitious so that it will take us
many years to come to terms with his vast achievement'
Colm Tóibín

'Bolaño continues to cast a spell, thanks to the wild metaphorical
reach of his tumbling sentences, his implausibly encyclopaedic
grasp of global affairs and the seductive sense that
twentieth-century history is a nightmarish riddle to
which only literature is the solution'
Guardian

'Latin American letters (wherever it may reside) has never had a
greater, more disturbing avenging angel than Bolaño'
Junot Díaz

'Bolaño was a flat-out genius, one of the greatest
writers of our time'
Paul Auster

ALSO BY ROBERTO BOLAÑO

NOVELS

The Savage Detectives

2666

Nazi Literature in the Americas

The Skating Rink

The Third Reich

Woes of the True Policeman

The Spirit of Science Fiction

NOVELLAS

By Night in Chile

Distant Star

Amulet

Antwerp

Monsieur Pain

A Little Lumpen Novelita

STORIES

Last Evenings on Earth

The Insufferable Gaucho

The Return

POETRY

The Romantic Dogs

Tres

The Unknown University

ROBERTO BOLAÑO

COWBOY GRAVES

THREE NOVELLAS

TRANSLATED FROM THE SPANISH BY
Natasha Wimmer

VINTAGE CLASSICS

1 3 5 7 9 10 8 6 4 2

Vintage Classics is part of the Penguin Random House
group of companies whose addresses can be found
at global.penguinrandomhouse.com

Penguin
Random House
UK

This edition published in Vintage Classics in 2024
First published in Spain with the title *Sepulcros de vaqueros* by Alfaguara in 2017
First published in the United States of America with the title
Cowboy Graves by Penguin Press in 2021

Designed by Amanda Dewey

penguin.co.uk/vintage-classics

Printed and bound in Great Britain by Clays Ltd, Elcograf S.p.A.

The authorised representative in the EEA is Penguin Random House Ireland,
Morrison Chambers, 32 Nassau Street, Dublin D02 YH68

A CIP catalogue record for this book is available from the British Library

ISBN 9781784879440

Penguin Random House is committed to a sustainable future
for our business, our readers and our planet. This book is made
from Forest Stewardship Council® certified paper.

CONTENTS

COWBOY
GRAVES

1.

The Airport

My name is Arturo and the first time I saw an airport was in 1968. It was November or December, maybe the end of October. I was fifteen then and I didn't know whether I was Chilean or Mexican and I didn't care much either way. We were going to Mexico to live with my father.

We tried to leave twice. The first time we didn't make it and the second time we did. The first time, as my mother and sister were talking to my grandmother and two or three other people I've forgotten, a stranger came up and gave me a book. I know that I saw his face—I scanned the whole length of him because he was so tall—and he smiled and made a motion (at no point did he say a word), inviting me to accept his unexpected gift. I've forgotten his face, too. He had bright eyes (though sometimes I see him wearing dark glasses that hide not just his eyes but most of his face) and smooth skin, tight around the ears, immaculately shaved. Then he was gone, and I remember sitting on one of the suitcases and reading the book. It was an international public airport manual. From it, I learned that an airport has hangars that are rented to different airlines for storage and maintenance; passenger terminals connected by air bridges to plane parking areas; a meteorological office; a control tower usually at least one hundred feet tall; emergency services located in special units on the landing field and controlled by the tower; a wind sock (which is a visual guide for gauging wind direction—when horizontal, it indicates that the wind speed is twenty-five to thirty knots); a flight operations building containing the main flight planning offices; a cargo center; shops; restaurants; and a police headquarters where it wouldn't be uncommon to run into an Interpol agent or two. Then we said goodbye to the people who had come to see us off and we got in the boarding line. I had the book in the pocket of my jacket. Then a voice said my mother's name over a loudspeaker. I think the whole airport heard it. The line stopped and the passengers looked around, searching for the woman who had been called. I looked around too, searching, but I knew who to search for so I looked straight at my mother, and to this day, as I write this, I'm ashamed of having done that. My mother's reaction, meanwhile, was odd: she pretended not to know what was going on and she looked around too, as if searching for the same person everyone else was, but not as eagerly as the other passengers on the Santiago–Lima–Quito–Mexico City flight. For a second, I thought that she would get away with it, that if she didn't accept the inevitable then the inevitable wouldn't happen, that so long as she kept moving toward the plane, ignoring the call of the loudspeaker, the voice would stop searching or keep searching even as we were on our way to Mexico. Then the voice called her name again, and this time it called my sister's name too (my sister turned pale and then red as a tomato) and mine. In the distance, behind glass, I think I saw my grandmother, looking distressed or flushed, waving and pointing for some reason to the watch on her left wrist, as if to say that we had just enough time or that our time had run out. Then two Interpol agents appeared and asked us none too nicely to follow them. A few seconds before, my mother had said keep calm, kids, and when we had to follow the policemen she repeated it, while demanding to know what was going on (apparently addressing the policemen who were escorting us but actually speaking to nobody in particular), and saying they'd better not delay us because we were going to miss our flight. That was my mother.

My mother was Chilean and my father was Mexican and I was born in Chile and I had lived there all my life. Moving from our house in Chile to my father's house may have terrified me more than I was prepared to admit. Also, I was leaving without having done a lot of the things I wanted to do. I tried to see Nicanor Parra before I left. I tried to make love with Mónica Vargas. I remember it now and it makes me grit my teeth, or maybe I just remember myself and I see myself gritting my teeth. In those days planes were dangerous and at the same time a great adventure, real travel, but I had no opinion on the subject. None of my teachers had flown on a plane. Nor had any of my classmates. Some had made love for the first time, but none had flown. My mother used to say that Mexico was a wonderful country. Up until then, we had always lived in small provincial capitals in the south of Chile. Santiago, where we spent a few days before flying, seemed to me a metropolis of dreams and nightmares. Wait till you see Mexico City, said my mother. Sometimes I imitated the way Mexicans talked, I imitated the way my father talked (though I could hardly remember his voice), and the way people in Mexican movies talked. I imitated Enrique Guzmán and Miguel Aceves Mejía. My mother and my sister laughed and that was how we spent some long winter afternoons, though by the end I never thought it was as funny as it had been at first and I would slip away without telling anyone where I was going. I liked to go out walking in the country. Once I had a horse. Its name was Ruckus. My father sent the money to buy it. I can't remember where we lived then, maybe Osorno, maybe outside of Llanquihue. I remember that we had a yard with a shack used as a workshop by the former tenant and later fixed up as a kind of stable for my horse. We had chickens, two geese, and a dog, Duke, who became fast friends with Ruckus. In any case, whenever I went out riding, my mother or Celestina would say: take Duke, he'll protect you and he'll protect your horse. For a long time (almost my whole life) I didn't know what they meant or I misunderstood them. Duke was a big dog, but even so he was smaller than me and much smaller than my horse. He was the size of a German shepherd (though he certainly wasn't a purebred), white with light brown spots and floppy ears. Sometimes he vanished for days and then I was strictly forbidden to go out riding. Three or five days later, at most, he would come back skinnier than ever, with cowlike eyes, so thirsty he could drink half a bucket of water. A little while ago, during a nighttime bombing raid that ended up not amounting to much, I dreamed about Duke and Ruckus. Both of them were dead and I knew it. Duke, Ruckus, I called, come here and get in bed with me, there's plenty of room. In my dream (I realized this immediately, without waking up), I was putting on a Chilean accent just as I had once put on the accent from Mexican movies. But I didn't care. I just wanted my dog and my horse to come into my room of their own accord and spend the night with me.

My mother was a beautiful woman. She read a lot. When I was ten, I believed that she had read more than anyone else in our town, wherever that was, though actually she never had more than fifty books and what she really liked were astrology or fashion magazines. She bought books by mail, and I think that's how Nicanor Parra's *Poems and Antipoems* turned up at our house, or at least I can't see any other way it could've gotten there. I guess whoever packed up the books for my mother put it in by mistake. At our house the only poet anybody ever read was Pablo Neruda, so I kept the Parra book for myself. My mother used to recite Neruda's twenty love poems (before or after my Mexican impersonations) and sometimes the three of us ended up crying and other times—only a few, I admit—the

7

blood rose to my face and I yelled and escaped out the window, feeling sick and ready to vomit. My mother, I remember, read like a Uruguayan poet I had heard once on the radio. The poet's name was Alcira Soust Scaffo, and just like me trying to imitate the way Mexicans talked, my mother tried to imitate the voice of Madame Soust Scaffo, which could swoop in a heartbeat from shrill peaks of despair to velvety depths. On a few horrific nights, my sister did a Marisol imitation, so as not to be left out. Sometimes I think about Chile and I think that all Chileans, at least those of us who are alive and who were more or less conscious in the sixties, deep down wanted to be impersonators. I remember a comedian who became famous for impersonating Batman and Robin. I remember that I collected Batman and Robin comics and I thought his impersonations were crude and sacrilegious, but I still laughed, and later I changed my mind and I didn't think they were so crude and sacrilegious anymore, just sad. One time Alcira Soust Scaffo came through Cauquenes or Temuco, or near where we lived, one more stop on a long tour of theaters in the south of Chile, and my mother took us to see her. She was very old (though on the few posters that we saw in the Plaza de Armas and around the town hall, she looked young and serious, with a hairstyle that must have been fashionable in the forties) and her voice, heard live without the kindly mediation of the radio, made me nervous from the start. This evening of verse was interrupted several times, I still don't know why, maybe for health reasons. After each interruption, Alcira Soust Scaffo returned to the stage whooping with laughter. My mother told me that she died soon afterward in a mental hospital in the city where she was from. After that, I couldn't stand Neruda. At school back then, they called me the Mexican. Sometimes it was a nice nickname to have, but other times it was more like an insult. I preferred to be called El Loco.

My mother worked a lot. I don't know whether she was good or bad at her job, but every two or three years she was transferred to a new post and a new province. And so we made the rounds of the records departments (generally just a euphemism for the hospital's main office, often small and dilapidated) at all the hospitals in the south of Chile. She was an ace at math. My mother, I mean. And she knew it, too: I'm an ace at math, she would say with a smile, but in a distracted kind of way. Because of math she had met my father in a six-month accelerated (or advanced or intensive) statistics course in Mexico. She came back to Chile pregnant, and soon I was born. Then my father came to visit Chile to meet me, and when he left, my mother was pregnant with my sister. I never liked math. I liked train trips, I liked bus trips and staying up all night, I liked to explore new houses where we lived, but I didn't like new schools. There was a bus line called Vía-Sur that ran down the Pan-American Highway to Puerto Montt. When I was little, I lived in Puerto Montt though now I can't remember anything about it, except maybe the rain. I also lived in Temuco, Valdivia, Los Ángeles, Osorno, Llanquihue, Cauquenes. I saw my father twice, once when I was eight and again when I was twelve. According to my mother, it was four times, but the two times I've forgotten must have been when I was very little, before I can remember. Vía-Sur probably doesn't exist anymore or the name has changed. There was also a bus line called Lit and one called the Fifth Horseman and even one called La Andina, whose logo was a mountain on fire—not a volcano, as you might expect, but a flaming mountain. Each time we moved, my father followed us like a ghost, from town to town, with his clumsy letters, with his promises. My mother, of course, had seen him more than four times in fifteen or sixteen years. Once she went to Mexico and they spent two months together, leaving me and my sister in the care of our Mapuche housekeeper. Back then we lived in Llanquihue. When my grandmother, who lived in Viña del Mar, found out that my mother had been too proud to leave us with her, she didn't speak to her for almost a year. My grandmother saw my father as the personification of vice and irresponsibility and she always referred to him as *that Mexican gentleman* or *that Mexican person*. In the end, my grandmother forgave my mother because, just as she believed my father was vice personified, she knew that my mother was an incurable dreamer.

The name of the housekeeper we stayed with was Celestina Maluenda and she was from Santa Bárbara in the province of Bío-Bío. For many years, she lived with us and followed my mother from province to province and house to house, until the day my mother decided that we were moving to Mexico. What happened then? I don't know. Maybe my mother asked her to come with us to Mexico and Celestina didn't want to leave; maybe my mother said so long, Celestina, old friend, it's over, we're done; maybe Celestina had children or grandchildren of her own to take care of and she thought the time had come; maybe my mother had no money to buy her a ticket to Mexico. My sister loved her and when they said goodbye, she cried. Celestina didn't cry: she stroked her hair and said take care. Me, she didn't even shake my hand. We glanced at each other, and she muttered something between her teeth, in her usual way. Maybe she said: take care of your sister, Arturo. Or maybe she cursed me. Maybe she wished me good luck.

Around the time we stayed alone with Celestina, we were living in Llanquihue, on the edge of town, on a street with no houses, lined with poplars and eucalyptus trees. We had a shotgun that somebody had left there (nobody knew who, though I suspected it was a friend of my mother's) and at night, before I went to bed, I would make the rounds of the house, going room by room, basement included, with the shotgun slung over my shoulder, followed by Celestina, who shone her flashlight into the corners. Sometimes, in an excess of zeal, I went out to patrol the yard, even venturing down the dark street. I made it to the first streetlight—a long way from the house—alone with the dog, and then I came back. Celestina would stand in the doorway, waiting for me. Then we shared a cigarette and went to bed. The shotgun was always under my bed. One night, though, I realized it wasn't loaded. When I asked Celestina who had taken the cartridges, she said that she had, as a precaution, so I wouldn't hurt anyone. Don't you realize that a gun is no good if it's not loaded? I said. It's good for scaring people, said Celestina. The whole thing infuriated me and I yelled at her, even cried to get the cartridges back. Swear that you won't kill anyone, Celestina said. Do you think I'm a murderer? I asked. I would only shoot in self-defense, to protect you and my sister. I don't need anyone to protect me with a gun, she said. So what if a killer comes one night? What would you do then? I'd run, holding you (*usted*, she said, addressing me formally, as she sometimes did) by one hand and your sister by the other. Finally I did swear, and Celestina gave me back the cartridges. When I had the shotgun loaded, I told her to put an apple on her head. You're wrong if you think I can't shoot straight, I said. Celestina looked at me for a long time without saying anything, her gaze deep and sad, and she said that at this rate I would end up a murderer. I don't kill birds, I said. I'm not a fucking hunter. I don't kill animals. It's just self-defense. Another time, my mother went on a trip to Miami with a group from the hospital and met up with my father there. Those were the thirty most wonderful days of my life, she said. Thank goodness you didn't get pregnant again, I said. My mother tried to hit me but I was too fast and dodged her.

Sometimes my mother paid her own way and other times my father sent her a plane ticket. He never sent tickets for us. According to my mother, it wasn't because he didn't want to see us but because he was scared of airplanes, afraid that the plane would crash and my sister and I would be found much later, sleeping in a nest of twisted steel, burned to a crisp in some lost American mountain range. Back then, I had serious doubts about this explanation. In the days between our first failed attempt to fly to Mexico and the second, my mother recalled my doubts and showed me (only me) the last letter my father had sent, after we'd made our travel plans. In the letter, my father said he slept with a gun in the drawer of his bedside table, in case of a crash. What does that mean? I asked. Your father is saying that he's prepared to shoot himself if anything happens to us. What could happen to us? The plane might go down, God forbid. My father plans to kill himself if we die? Yes, said my mother, when he says he sleeps with a gun by his side, he means that he plans to kill himself if anything happens to you. By *you* she meant me and my sister. For days, I couldn't get the idea of my father and his gun out of my head. Even after we made it to Mexico and before I started at a new Mexican school, when I didn't have anything to do and I didn't know anybody, I went looking for the gun in every room of the house, but I never found it.

We did get letters, long letters in terrible handwriting with lots of spelling mistakes. In them, he talked about "my adopted country," as he pompously referred to Chile, or "my other country," "my Chilean self," "my other self." Sometimes, though not often, he talked about my grandfather, who was Spanish, from Galicia, and about my Sonoran Indian grandmother, who seemed as remote as aliens to me. He said that he was the youngest of seven children, that my grandfather was ninety and owned land near Santa Teresa, and that my grandmother was sixty, exactly thirty years younger than my grandfather. Sometimes, when I was bored, I made calculations (though I hated math) and the numbers didn't add up: according to my mother, who knew and liked to report everyone's age except her own, my father was twenty-five when I was born; therefore, he must have been forty around the time we moved to Mexico. If my grandmother was sixty, that meant she was twenty when she had my father; but if my father was the youngest of seven children, how old could my grandmother have been when she gave birth to her first? Assuming that she'd had them one after another, she might have been thirteen, two years younger than me and one year younger than my sister. My grandmother, thirteen; my grandfather, forty-three. Of course, there was another possibility: my grandmother wasn't the mother of all my grandfather's children; just the last two, or just my father. According to my father's horrible letters, which I sometimes didn't even finish reading, until recently my grandfather could still get up on a horse. My father also said that when he talked to my grandfather on the phone, telling him how he'd sent money for a horse for me—though here he got his verb tenses mixed up, and nothing about the story quite made sense—the old man said that he hoped to see me ride someday in Sonora, on a real Sonoran horse. All this did was turn me against my grandfather, and anyway I never met him. Once I asked my father (casually, as if we were talking about soccer, when we were stuck in a traffic jam on Insurgentes) about my grandmother's precocious motherhood and then he confessed that she was my grandfather's second wife. She'd had her first child at nineteen and the second (and last) at twenty. For some reason, then I asked about his first wife (my father's, not my grandfather's), with no transition or preamble, as if everything we'd talked about that afternoon had been leading up to this point. At first my father was cool and quiet, staring forward with his hands on the wheel. Then he said that in Mexico, unlike in Chile, divorce had been possible for a long time, but it cost a lot, which was not the case in Chile. I don't know why, he said, but it's expensive to split up. It must be because of the fucking kids, I said, and I threw the cigarette out the window (ever since I'd turned fifteen, from the time I'd set foot in Mexico City, my father had let me smoke). That must be it, he said. I can't remember anymore whether we were heading toward UNAM or toward La Villa, just that we were crawling along and my father didn't look at me for a while (he was staring at the motionless crush of cars—*carros*, as they call them in Mexico—on the avenue, but by his expression he might have been gazing out over the great open spaces of America, the dive bars and factories, the shadowy buildings where men like him lived, men past forty), but when he did look at me, he smiled and started to speak, but in the end he didn't say anything.

The last time my father was in Chile, a year and a half before we left for Mexico, some friends of my mother's invited us to their country house for the weekend. One afternoon we went riding. Some days I remember it clearly—the voices; the yellows and dark greens; the birds; the scattered clouds, incredibly high—and other days I remember it wreathed in fog, like some jumpy or distorted movie, or like somebody did something to my brain. There were seven of us Chileans and one Mexican, and the Chileans wanted to see if the Mexican was man enough to ride fast and not fall off the horse (I was one of the Chileans and I wanted to see too). I suspect that one of the Chileans, a doctor—though for all that it matters, he might have been a nurse—had slept with my mother, I remember him over at our house, my mother's voice ordering Celestina to put us to bed, the music coming from the record player when they were alone, the soundtrack from *Black Orpheus*. I also remember the doctor's (or nurse's) sadness and occasional moodiness, though even at his moodiest he wouldn't budge from my mother's side in the hectic days before my father's arrival. So my mother's morose friend was there, and I was there, and five other Chileans, and I remember that they were drinking Maule wine and as we got farther from the big house I remember some jokes too, some allusions to the equestrian art in the two sister countries (which is a manner of speaking, since Chile and Mexico have nothing in common, except that one is at the top of Latin America and the other is at the bottom, the head and the tail of the subcontinent, but which is the head and which the tail depends on who's looking or who's suffering, and neither position is advantageous). (Actually, no Latin American country is in an advantageous position. We're all on the slopes of the mountain, all at the bottom of the ravine. What ravine?

The Yuro Ravine.) The point is, we were riding. Earlier, at the stables, my father had wanted to saddle his horse himself, then he checked my horse's cinch, bridle, bit. He made a few remarks about the saddle, which he thought was showy. At first we began walking and the adults were drinking and laughing. I remember that we crossed a stream where my sister and I had swum in past summers. Then we came out into an empty field. On the other side of the fence, cows were grazing. Now two of the group, probably the older children of the country house's owner, broke into a gallop and jumped the fence. My father followed. My father was just a few years older and I suppose he considered it his duty as a guest to follow them. Or maybe there was an earlier challenge or bet involved, I don't know. All I know is that he went riding after them and I saw him reach the fence and jump it cleanly. Then I heard a cry, it was a bird, but I don't know what kind of bird, maybe a southern lapwing, or maybe it was the two brothers galloping toward the next fence, but to me it sounded like the cry of a condor, as if a giant vulture had come out of the woods that we had left and was flying over the fields, invisible and menacing. Just as my father was about to jump the second fence I galloped after him. I felt the horse quiver, felt its power, and I approached the first fence like a drunk man. From here the field began to slope downhill, and though the slope seemed gentle from a distance, with the tall grass swaying a little in the wind, on horseback and galloping it was uneven, rutted, steep. When I looked up, the two brothers had come to a halt and one of the horses was rearing up in fear, maybe there was a snake, I thought, and I was scared, or maybe the rider was angry and was making the horse rear up in punishment. My father, farther away, reached the third fence, and from behind I seemed to hear shouts. Someone, the owner of the house, was calling for him to stop; someone, the nurse, was shrieking like in a Miguel Aceves Mejía movie, a Jorge Negrete movie, a Pedro Infante or Antonio Aguilar movie, a Resortes and Calambres movie, shrieks of pain and joy, shrieks of heartbreak and freedom, I realized all of a sudden as the second fence approached, and I shouted too and clung with my legs as my horse floated over it like a sigh and we kept rushing downhill, my father had already disappeared down the slope and the two brothers were to my left and then behind me, one of them on the ground examining his horse's front hoof. Next came a steep rise and once I'd breasted it I could see a river walled with trees, and, a little farther off, a small wood, where some araucarias rose above the other trees. I didn't see my father or his horse anywhere. I jumped the third fence and galloped down toward the wood. Before I got there I slowed the horse to a walk. I found my father sitting on a stump with an unlit cigarette in his hand. The hand holding the cigarette was shaking. He was sweating heavily, his face was flushed, and he had unbuttoned several buttons of his shirt. Until I got off the horse, he didn't seem to notice my presence. I sat next to him on the ground and asked whether he'd had a good run. I don't know why I did it, he said, I could have broken my neck. Then he said: it's been a long time since I rode a horse. Far away, at the top of the hill, the others appeared; maybe somebody saw us and waved a hand; then they gestured, pointing toward a stretch along the river where the hill became less steep, the way they planned to go. I raised an arm to show I'd gotten the message. My father didn't look up. He'd lit his cigarette and was sweating even more profusely. For a moment I wondered whether he was crying. The other riders waved, signaling to me, and were swallowed up by the earth. I sat back down next to my father. At first the cigarette seemed to choke him. It was a Cabañas and he was used to Mexican Delicados, stronger but smoother (quality tobacco, basically), but then he started to blow distracted smoke rings, as if his lips didn't belong to him, staring first at the ground covered in twigs, sprigs of grass, clumps of dirt, and then gazing upward, perfect smoke rings of different sizes and even thicknesses. Then, after putting out his cigarette, my father said: do you want to hear how cowboys travel in Mexico? Dad, there are no cowboys in Mexico, I said. Of course there are, said my father, I used to be a cowboy and your grandfather was a cowboy, and even your grandmother was a cowboy. Do you know why I'm here, so far from everywhere? The question didn't seem fair to me, I lived here, so far from everywhere, and he seemed to be constantly forgetting that, but at the same time I imagined he was about to tell me something that would change my life. Because of my mother, I said. Yes, because of your mother, among other things, he said. Because of you and your sister, he said after a silence. Among other things. Then he was quiet, as if he'd suddenly forgotten what we had been talking about, and at the far edge of the wood the rest of the group appeared. My father got up and said that we should join them. All my life I've tried to be a sportsman, he said before getting on his horse, but I've never managed it.

My mother read mail-order romance novels sent from Santiago and she read paranormal magazines. My father read only westerns. I read Nicanor Parra and I thought that gave me an advantage. It gave me no advantage at all, of course. Which was more or less what Mónica Vargas told me a few days before I left Chile. Back then, toward the end of 1968, it wasn't easy to leave one Latin American country and enter another. Even today it's hard, but back then it was worse. You had to fill out a big stack of papers required for the trip, forms that couldn't be processed in the small provincial capital where we lived. So we sold everything we had, which wasn't much—some furniture, more or less—and two weeks before the date of our trip (our first attempt to leave the country) we moved to Santiago, where we stayed with one of my mother's friends, Rebeca Vargas, a high school teacher and southern transplant. She lived with her younger sister, Mónica Vargas, who was studying at the conservatory.

Mónica was very thin, with long, straight hair and big breasts, and she played the flute. The first night we spent there, we stayed up late talking, and when everyone had gone to bed and we were about to go to bed too (she in her sister's room and I on the sofa), we went out onto the balcony, maybe to look at the streetlights and the neon signs of Santiago, or to gaze at the mountains by the light of the moon, which looked like a reflector dangling in the abyss. Before that, in the living room or the kitchen, I remember helping her to make another round of tea and bread with avocado and jam (as if that night, my mother and all of us who had stayed up late listening to her talk had worked up an appetite: not for lunch or dinner, but for afternoon tea, which is the appetite of tales and legend), and when she asked me what I wanted to study in Mexico, I said medicine, but I really wanted to be a poet. That's great, she said, setting out the tea, the milk, the yogurt (it was the first time I'd had yogurt that way, in a container), with a Hilton firmly pinched between her lips or her long fingers with bitten nails. What have you read? The question came as such a surprise that suddenly I had no idea what to say, at a time in my life when I had answers for everything. Nicanor Parra, I said. Ah, Nicanor, said Mónica, as if she knew him and they were dear friends. *Poems and Antipoems*, Editorial Nascimento, 1954, I said. He's the only one worth reading, said Mónica, and that was it until we went out onto the balcony. She was holding a cigarette, her last of the night, and I was debating whether to ask her for one, afraid and embarrassed that she would say no because I wasn't old enough to smoke, though now I know that she wouldn't have. She was sitting in a wooden folding chair and I was standing, almost with my back to her, staring at the dark city, wishing I never had to leave. Then

Mónica said that she was going to loan me a book to read before we left. What book? I asked. Rilke, she said. *Letters to a Young Poet*. I remember that we looked at each other, or it seemed to me that we did—Mónica actually had her eyes fixed on the hazy mass of Santiago—and I remember that I felt as offended, as humiliated, as if she had refused me a cigarette. I realized that the *Letters* were her way of advising me not to write poetry; I realized that the *Young Poet* never wrote anything worthwhile, that at best he'd been killed in some duel or war; I realized that Mónica might talk like Nicanor was her friend but she had no idea how to read him; I realized that Mónica knew that aside from Nicanor Parra (*Mr.* Parra), I hadn't read much in my life. I realized all of this in a second, and I felt like crouching there on the balcony and saying: you're so right, but you couldn't be more wrong—not a very Chilean thing to say, though very Mexican. Instead I looked at her and asked for a cigarette. Silently, as if her thoughts were far from that balcony hanging innocently over Santiago, she handed me the pack and then gave me a light. We smoked for a while in silence. She finished hers (she smoked them down to the filter) and I smoked my whole cigarette. Then we shut the door to the balcony and I sat on the sofa waiting for her to leave so I could go to bed. Mónica vanished for a second and then she came back with the Rilke. If you're not too tired, start it tonight, she said. Then she said good night and I kissed her on the mouth. She didn't seem surprised, but she gave me a look of reproach before disappearing down the hallway. Actually, the hallway was small and the apartment was small, much smaller than the house we had just left, but unfamiliar places always seem bigger. The next night, when Mónica got back from her classes at the conservatory, I told her I thought the author of *Letters to a Young Poet* was a prude. That's all? she said, her expression as serious as it had been the night before. That's all, I said. That night, Mónica didn't hang around after dinner to smoke a last cigarette with me.

That night I had nightmares and slept badly. The next morning I asked my mother for money and I went to say goodbye to Nicanor Parra.

I didn't know where he lived, of course. From the Vargas sisters' place I called a publishing house and the dean's office at the University of Chile. Finally I got an address. From the start, I suspected that it would be hard to get there and just as hard to get back. I took a bus that dropped me at an intersection. Then I got on another bus. This one headed down narrow, winding streets full of stores and street vendors selling everything from aluminum pots and pans to toy soldiers. We navigated some roughly paved streets, then we came out into a vacant lot as big and flat as ten soccer fields, more or less surrounded by half-toppled brick walls. I got off there and continued on foot. Once I had left the vacant lot behind, the road forked. In one direction was a street with no buildings (it looked more like a country road than a street) and in the other was a neighborhood of single-story houses, with some unpaved streets and lots of children and dogs. I decided to follow the country road; other groups of houses soon appeared, looking flatter, more squashed or squat, a phenomenon that intensified as I got closer to the cordillera, as if the mountains or the air were crushing the houses to the ground. Then I came to a bus stop and asked for directions. People pointed me toward a street that ran uphill. That way, they said. I went up the street and ahead I saw a river and a bridge. I crossed over and made my way into a neighborhood of streets lined with larches. I saw a sign that said Lo Paigüe, and I guessed that was the name of the neighborhood. I went into a children's clothing store and said I was looking for Nicanor Parra's house. It's at the other end of Lo Paigüe, answered a woman. All right, I said, and I kept walking along the riverbank. Soon the river split into channels, some blocked by dams made of big cans full of mud and assorted trash. I went to get a closer look, and in the riverbed two rats stared up at me from a path of twigs and fossilized bottles linking the islands in the delta of wastewater. One of them, the skinnier one, smiled at me. A humble smile, as if to say: Here I am, Arturo, getting by, how's it going, man? I thought I was losing it but I stood motionless there on the bank between the path and the delta-turned-dump (though maybe it was the other way around: maybe as the dump grew, it had turned into a delta). The rat shot me a backward glance—over its shoulder, you might say—still with that smile of deep humility dripping from its snout, and then it followed its comrade down, leaping more whimsically than energetically (and not without a certain grace, radiating calm dignity). Across a dusty street, where some spindly apple and Japanese plum trees grew, was the house whose address I had written down on a piece of paper. From a garage set up as a workshop in the back came the sounds of chisel and handsaw. The house looked empty, with its drawn curtains, weedy yard, and general air of abandonment. I rang the bell and a man stuck his head out the open door of the garage. What do you want? I'm looking for Nicanor Parra, the poet, I said. Come in, he said. He was sitting on a little wicker stool and even when he beckoned me in he didn't rise, only tilted forward on the stool's front legs. When I was inside he looked me over and said that no poet lived there, though he could recite a poem for me if I wanted. He was about fifty, his hair longish and gray, with the look of an old hustler or a singer. I showed him the paper with the address on it. He read it a few times and said no, I had the wrong address. But did Nicanor Parra used to live here? I asked. A poet did live in the neighborhood, he said, but I don't know if I'd go so far as to say it was Parra, no. Do you want a glass of wine, my friend, or are you too young for that? I accepted mostly just to put off the ride back for a few minutes, since I sensed it would be long and dull. What do you make? I asked, sitting down on another wicker stool. Guitars, he said. I make guitars, though not very good ones, to be honest. Do they sell? Not very well, but I make ends meet. For a while, the two of us were silent as he sanded a shapeless piece of wood, or at least that's what it looked like to me, since I know nothing about guitars. In a few days I'm going to Mexico, I said. Ah, he said, in search of new shores, are you? Yes, I said. Things are turning ugly in these parts, he said, though in Mexico, not to say things are bad, but they probably aren't much better, are they? My father is Mexican, I said. Good thing to have a father, he said, let's drink to that. We clinked glasses. To the dads, he said, wherever they are. I shook my head in what was meant to be an incredulous way, as if to say: I get the joke, but I don't share the sentiment. Do you live here? I asked. No, he said, I just have my workshop here, a friend rents it to me for next to nothing, but I live on the other side of the river. The Lo Paigüe River? I asked. That's the one, he said, Avenida Manuel Rodríguez, number 353, you're very welcome there. I used to live in the South, I said, not sure why I was saying it. So what brings you here to say goodbye to Parra the poet, if you don't mind me asking, he said. Nothing in particular, I said, I'm a poet too and I thought . . . Man! he said, a poet! Then I really will recite that poem for you, to see what you think. I was quiet, waiting. He picked up a guitar to accompany himself and began. His voice was gravelly but warm.

Like the queen of the poooor
In jeeeans
long Jesus haaair
kniiife in the pocket
crude flower tattoooo

I was halfway throoough
my miserable liiife
when yooou turned up
flower of the gutter, flower of the diiirt
and I was saaaved.
Like the queen of the poooor.

Nice, I said, looking out the garage door at the passing clouds. It's not bad, agreed the man, I wrote it three months ago, at La Gorda Martínez's. After a dreamy silence, he added: where they make a tomato salsa that's finger-licking good. Then the guitar maker began talking about trips to the Chilean interior as if it were a faraway, exotic country, and about singer-songwriters, pimps, and whores. But I always come back to the shop, he said at last. Before I left, he recited another of his poems for me.

Tempus fugit, darlin'
said the old man to his ladyyy
sittin' on the edge of the abyss
as the light was fadin'
scraps of memoryyy
come back, come a-flittin'
torn photographs
oh how we wanted
to set life on fire
dressin' the sky in tatters

Later he walked out to the street with me and showed me the way to a bus stop. We shook hands and I headed off. On a hill I saw two children playing with a metal hoop. I imagined that if I stepped through the hoop, like a trained pig, I would come out in another dimension. That night, I told Mónica everything that had happened to me and I returned the Rilke book. The next day, we went to the movies with my grandmother, who had come to Santiago to see us off and was staying with some relatives until the day of our departure—our first aborted attempt and then also the second (successful) one—though until the plane was in the air I wasn't convinced we'd be able to leave the country. The rest of my memories are confused. I think I wrote a letter to Mónica (I don't dare call it a poem) that I later ripped up, then I got my first passport and we went to the movies a few more times.

And here we are back at the airport, and my mother, followed with enormous effort by my sister and me, both of us dragging suitcases that we're trying to pass off as carry-on luggage, are taken to the Interpol offices. And I remember that everybody was staring at us and that as I became conscious of being watched I was thinking two things: first, that if I'd had my gun (the shotgun that had turned up mysteriously at our house and that I now think belonged to one of my mother's lovers), I would have shot at the police and then set fire to the airport; second, that they would never let us leave Chile, which meant that my fate was never to see anything or be seen. And then my mother sparred (verbally) with the policemen, and if

28

she was afraid of being arrested, she managed to hide it very skillfully, and she insulted a creditor from the lands that we were leaving behind with the elegance and disdain of someone who practically lived on planes (the phrase *jet set* had begun to appear frequently in the magazines that she read), hopping from capital to great world capital. And then, assuming the voice of a woman in distress, she asked for a favor, from one Chilean to another. And then she even begged to be allowed to leave, saying that the father of her children was expecting her and he was the kind of man who might commit some foolish act at the slightest provocation. But nothing could be done and that night we weren't able to get on a plane (there was some claim about an unpaid bill, that was all) and once we'd gotten over the shock we returned to the Vargas sisters' place with my grandmother (who spent the night there too) and Rebeca Vargas (soothing my frantic mother, what a good friend she was) and one or two other people I can't remember now. And Mónica was there. She didn't like goodbyes and she probably had better things to do than go to the airport with some southerners she'd likely never see again, so she made us tell the whole story over, and despite the laughter, that was a sad night. More than sad: black, gloomy, sleepless. And when everyone had gone to bed, I sat out on the balcony in shirtsleeves, freezing to death, with the Parra book unopened in my hands. And when everything seemed most hopeless, my mother had an asthma attack.

2

The Grub

He looked like a grub, with his straw hat and a Bali hanging from his lower lip. Every morning, I'd see him sitting on a bench in the Alameda as I went into the Librería de Cristal to browse, and when I raised my head, looking out through the bookstore wall, which really was made of glass, there he was, stock-still, staring into space.

I guess we ended up getting used to each other. I'd show up at eight-thirty in the morning and he'd be there already, sitting on a bench, just smoking and staring into space. I never saw him with a newspaper, a sandwich, a beer. Once, watching him from the French literature shelves, I imagined he must sleep in the Alameda on a bench, or in some doorway on a nearby street, but then I decided that he was too clean to be sleeping on the street and he must have a room in a boarding-house. He was a creature of habit, like me, I observed. I got up early, ate breakfast with my mother, father, and sister, pretended that I was going to school, and took a bus to the center of the city, where I devoted the first half of the morning to books and walking around and the second half to movies and sex.

I usually bought books at the Librería de Cristal and the Librería el Sótano. If I was short of money, then it was the former, where there was always a bargain table. If I was flush, then it was the latter. If I had no money, I stole indiscriminately from one or the other, slipping a book or two among my text-books. Either way, a visit to the Librería de Cristal and the Librería el Sótano (across from the Alameda and located in a basement, as the name indicates) was mandatory. Sometimes I arrived before the stores opened and then I would stop at a sandwich cart, buy a ham sandwich and a cup of mango juice, and wait. Sometimes—after my amazing breakfast—I wrote. All of this went on until ten, which was when some of the movie houses had their first show of the day. I preferred European movies, though some inspired mornings I would take my chances on new Mexican cinema.

It was a French movie I saw the most, I think. Two girls live alone in a house in the middle of nowhere. The blonde has split up with her boyfriend and, on top of that (on top of her suffering, I mean), she has personality problems: she thinks she's in love with her friend. The redhead is younger, more innocent, more irresponsible; in other words, she's happier (though I was young, innocent, and irresponsible back then and I was convinced that I was deeply unhappy). One day, a fugitive sneaks into the house and takes them captive. The funny thing is that the break-in happens on the very night that the blonde has decided to make love with the redhead and then commit suicide. The fugitive gets in through a window, creeps around the house with a knife in his hand, comes into the redhead's bedroom, tackles her, ties her up, interrogates her, asks how many other people live in the house. The redhead says it's just her and the blonde, and he gags her. But the blonde isn't in her room and the fugitive looks all over the house, getting more and more nervous, until finally he finds her on the basement floor, out cold, evidently having swallowed a whole medicine cabinet full of pills. The fugitive isn't a killer, or anyway he doesn't kill women, and he saves the blonde: he makes her throw up, brews her a pot of coffee, etcetera. Then the days go by and the women and the fugitive begin to grow close. The fugitive tells them his story: he's an ex-con, an ex–bank thief, his wife has left him. The women are cabaret dancers and one afternoon or night (nobody knows exactly what time it is since they've been keeping the curtains drawn), they put on a play: the blonde wraps herself in a magnificent bearskin and the redhead pretends to be an animal tamer. At first the bear obeys, but then it rebels and little by little it tears the clothes off the redhead with its claws. At last she falls in defeat, naked, and the bear is on top of her. No, it doesn't kill her; it makes love to her. And here comes the strangest part: after watching this act, the fugitive falls in love with the blonde, not the redhead; in other words, the bear. The ending is predictable but poetic: one rainy night, after the fugitive kills two ex-comrades, he and the blonde flee to parts unknown and the redhead is left sitting in an armchair, reading, giving them a head start before she calls the police. The book the redhead is reading, I realized the third time I saw the movie, is Camus's *The Fall*. I also saw some Mexican movies of more or less the same type: beautiful women who are kidnapped by criminal types; escaped prisoners who snatch rich girls and at the end of a night of passion are riddled with bullets; beautiful maids who start from zero and reach the zenith of wealth and power. Back then almost all movies made in Mexico were erotic thrillers, though there was some erotic horror and erotic comedy too. The horror movies followed the classic line of Mexican horror established in the fifties, as emblematic of my new country's culture as the muralist painters. Featuring the Saint, the Mad Scientist, the Vampire Cowboy, or the Innocent Girl, they were seasoned with modern nudes (preferably unknown American or European actresses or the occasional Argentine ingenue), explicit sex scenes, and a cruelty bordering on the risible and the unforgivable. Erotic comedy wasn't my thing.

One morning, as I was looking for a book in the Librería el Sótano, I saw that a scene from a film was being shot and I went over to investigate. I recognized Jacqueline Andere. It was the first time I'd seen one of my movie legends in person.

When I went to the movies alone I would sit in the front row and cross my legs. With my left hand I rubbed my penis through my pants until I came. The only problem was syncing my orgasms with the best scenes in the movie, which wasn't so hard when I was seeing something for the second or third time, but could be truly agonizing on a first viewing. When I saw *Barbarella*, for example, I came right away (during the strip-tease in the spaceship) and when I saw *Crimenes pasionales* with an actress of Jacqueline Andere's generation—totally gorgeous, one of my favorites, though I've forgotten her name—I put off coming for so long that it finally happened as the credits were rolling. My assiduous moviegoing gave me so much practice that in the end I became an expert in inscrutable masturbation and motionless orgasms (face frozen, maybe just a drop of sweat rolling down my cheek); the movements of my left hand were so precise and economical that today it strikes me as in-credible. But anyway, that morning I spotted Jacqueline Andere and I had the dumb idea to go and ask for her autograph. I don't know why; I'd never been interested in autographs. So when she finished shooting her scene I went up to her (it was a surprise to discover how short she was, even in her stiletto heels) and asked if I could get her autograph. It was one of the simplest things I've ever done. Nobody stopped me, nobody came between Jacqueline and me, nobody asked what I was doing there. For a second I thought that I could have kid-napped Jacqueline. Just the prospect of it made my hair stand on end. In the scene, she was walking along a path in the Alameda. When she was done, she stopped for a moment, as if she'd heard something, though none of the crew had said anything to her, and then she walked on toward the Palacio de Bellas Artes, where years later I would give a disastrous poetry reading (disastrous because of what happened at it and after it), and all I had to do was walk toward her. When I reached her, I stopped. She looked me up and down, her blond hair an ashy color that I had never seen before (it might have been dyed), her eyes big, almond shaped, sweet—but no, *sweet* isn't the word; calm, incredibly calm, as if she was drugged or had flatlined or was an alien—and she said something that I didn't understand.

The pen, she said, the pen to sign with.

I found a pen in my jacket pocket and I had her sign the first page of Camus's *The Fall*. Are you a student? she asked. Yes, I said. So why are you here instead of in class? She didn't say it in an aggressive way and she wasn't being sarcastic; she was just stating a fact. Sometimes I take the morning off, I said. Actually, I had been taking every morning off for months now, and I knew I wouldn't be going back to class, though I preferred to postpone the reckoning, the moment when I would have to tell my parents. She asked my name. All right, then, let's sign, she said. Then she smiled at me, shook my hand (her hand was small, delicate boned), and walked off across the Alameda alone. I stood there watching her. Two women approached her fifty yards farther along. They looked like missionary nuns, two Mexican missionary nuns in Africa, pausing there with Jacqueline under an ahuehuete, and then the three of them walked off toward Bellas Artes.

On the first page of *The Fall*, Jacqueline wrote: "For Arturo Belano, a liberated student, with a kiss from Jacqueline Andere." When I read it I couldn't help laughing. Suddenly I wasn't in the mood for bookstores, long walks, reading, early shows (especially early shows). The prow of an enormous cloud appeared in the center of Mexico City, while to the north of the city the first thunder echoed and lightning split the sky. I realized suddenly that the filming had been cut short because it was about to rain. I felt lonely, and for a few seconds I was afraid and I wished frantically to be back home. Then the Grub waved to me. I suppose after all this time he had noticed me too. I turned and there he was, sitting on the same bench as always, distinct, absolutely real in his straw hat and white shirt. When the film crew left, I noted fearfully, it was as if the sea had parted. The empty Alameda was the ocean bottom and the Grub its most precious jewel. I greeted him, probably made some banal remark, and we headed out of the Alameda together into the neighborhood around the Blanquita Theater.

What happened next is hazy and at the same time sharp, hyperreal. The bar was called Las Camelias. I ordered enchiladas and a Tecate, the Grub a Coca-Cola, and later (but it couldn't have been much later) he bought two turtle eggs from a street vendor. We talked about Jacqueline Andere. It wasn't long before I realized, astounded, that he didn't know she was an actress. I pointed out that she had been filming just now, but the Grub simply didn't remember the crew or the equipment set up for the shoot. Then it stopped raining and the Grub pulled a wad of bills out of his back pocket, paid, and left.

The next day we saw each other again. By his expression, I thought that he didn't recognize me or didn't want to say hello. Still, I felt indebted to him and I went up to him. He seemed to be asleep with his eyes open. He was thin, but except for his arms and legs, his flesh looked soft, even flabby. His flaccidity was more moral than physical. His bones were small and strong. Soon I learned that he was from the North or he had lived in the North for a long time, which is essentially the same thing. I'm from Sonora, he said. I thought that was funny, since my grandfather was from there too. This interested the Grub, and he wanted to know what part of Sonora. Santa Teresa, I said. I'm from Villaviciosa, said the Grub. One night I asked my father if he had heard of Villaviciosa. Of course I've heard of it, said my father, it's a few miles from Santa Teresa. I asked him to describe it to me. It's a very small town, my father said, the population can't be over a thousand (later I learned that it wasn't even five hundred), the people are poor, no way to make a living, not a single industry. It's fated to disappear, said my father. Disappear how? I asked. Emigration, said my father, people leaving for cities like Santa Teresa or Hermosillo or heading to the United States. When I told the Grub this, he didn't agree, though in reality words like *agree* or *disagree* meant nothing to him: the Grub never argued about anything, nor did he express opinions. He was no model of respect for others. He listened and registered information, or maybe he just listened and then forgot, trapped in a different orbit. His voice was soft and monotonous though sometimes it rose in pitch and then he seemed like a lunatic imitating a lunatic and I never knew whether he did it on purpose, as part of a game that only he understood, or whether he just couldn't help himself and those shrill moments were part of the hell he was living. He ascribed his confidence in Villaviciosa to the town's longevity, and also (though I realized this later) to the precariousness that engulfed it and ate away at it—the very thing that threatened its existence, according to my father. He wasn't a curious person, though few things got past him. Once he looked at the books I had with me, one by one, as if reading was a chore. Then he never showed any interest in my books again, though each morning I appeared with a new one. Occasionally—maybe because he considered me a fellow countryman somehow—we talked about Sonora, which I hardly knew: I had been there only once, for my grandfather's funeral. He named towns like Nacozari, Bacoache, Fronteras, Villa Hidalgo, Bacerac, Bavispe, Agua Prieta, Naco, which gleamed like gold in my mind. He named lost villages in the municipalities of Nácori Chico and Bacadéhuachi, near the border with the state of Chihuahua, and then—I don't know why—he covered his mouth, like someone about to sneeze or yawn. He seemed to have walked and slept in every mountain range: Las Palomas and La Cieneguita, Sierra Guijas and Sierra La Madera, Sierra San Antonio and Sierra Cibuta, Sierra Tumacacori and Sierra Sierrita (well over the Arizona border), Sierra Cuevas and Sierra Ochitahueca to the northeast near Chihuahua, Sierra La Pola and Sierra Las Tablas to the south on the way to Sinaloa, Sierra La Gloria and Sierra El Pinacate to the northeast, in the direction of Baja California. He had been all over Sonora, from Huatabampo and Empalme on the Gulf of California, to the lost hamlets in the desert or the mountains, near Arizona. He could speak Yaqui and Papago (which flowed freely in Sonora and Arizona) and he could understand Seri, Pima, Mayo, and English. His Spanish was flat, sometimes with a faint put-on air belied by his eyes.

I've been walking like a lost soul on the lands of your grandfather, may he rest in peace, he said to me once.

We met each morning. Sometimes I tried to pretend I'd forgotten, maybe go back to my solitary walks, my morning movie sessions, but he was always there, sitting on a bench in the Alameda, very still, with the Bali hanging from his lips and his straw hat covering half his forehead (his grub's forehead). Deep in the shelves of the Librería de Cristal, I couldn't help seeing him, watching him for a while, and finally going to sit down next to him.

It wasn't long before I discovered that the Grub was always

armed. At first I thought that maybe he was a cop or someone was after him, but it was obvious he wasn't a cop (or wasn't a cop anymore) and I've never met anyone less concerned about the people around him: he never glanced behind him, never looked to either side, hardly ever looked down. When I asked why he carried a weapon, the Grub replied that it was a habit and I believed him immediately. He wore the pistol on his back, between his spine and his pants. Have you used it many times? I asked him. Yes, many times, he said as if in a dream. For days I was obsessed with the Grub's gun. It made me uncomfortable to be sitting on a bench in the Alameda talking (or monologizing) to an armed man, not because of what he might do to me, because from the very beginning I knew that the Grub and I would always be friends—but for fear the Mexico City police would spot us, for fear they would frisk us and find the Grub's gun and the two of us would end up in a cell at the station.

One morning, he got sick and talked to me about Villaviciosa. I spotted him from the Librería de Cristal and he looked the same as usual to me, but when I got close I saw that his shirt was wrinkled as if he'd slept in it, and when I sat down next to him, I noticed that he was shaking uncontrollably. You have a fever, I said, you have to get in bed. Despite his protests, I went with him to the boardinghouse where he lived. Lie down, I said. The Grub took off his shirt, put the pistol under his pillow, and seemed to fall asleep instantly, though with his open eyes fixed on the ceiling. In the room, there was a narrow bed, a night table, a dilapidated wardrobe. In the wardrobe, I saw three perfectly folded white shirts and two pairs of white pants hanging on their respective hangers. Under the bed was a leather briefcase of excellent quality, the kind that has a combination lock like a strongbox. I didn't see a single newspaper or magazine. The place smelled of disinfectant. Give me money to go to the pharmacy to buy you something, I said. He handed me a roll of bills from his pants pocket and was still again. Every so often a tremor shook him from head to foot as if he was about to die. For a moment, I thought that maybe it would be best to call a doctor, but I realized the Grub wouldn't like that. When I came back, loaded down with medicine and bottles of Coca-Cola, he had gone to sleep. I gave him a massive dose of antibiotics and some pills to bring his fever down. Then I made him drink half a liter of Coca-Cola. I had also bought him a pancake, which I left on the night table in case he was hungry later. When I was about to go, he opened his eyes and started to talk about Villaviciosa.

In his own peculiar way, he was lavish with detail. He said that the town had sixty houses at most, two bars, a grocery store. He said that the houses were adobe and some yards were paved. He said that the town was two or three thousand years old and its natives made a living as hired killers and bodyguards. He said that a river ran nearby. It was called Río Negro because of the color of its waters, and where it ran past the cemetery, it became a delta that was sucked down into the dry earth. He said that people sometimes spent a long time gazing at the horizon, at the sun setting behind the Lagarto Mountains, and that the horizon was flesh colored, like a dying man's back. What do they think they'll see? I asked. I don't know, he said. Then he said: a cock. And then: wind and dust, maybe. Then he seemed to relax and after a while I decided that he was asleep. I'll be back tomorrow, I whispered. Take your medicine and stay in bed. The next morning, before stopping by the Grub's boardinghouse, I spent a while at the Librería de Cristal, as usual. When I was about to go, I saw him through the transparent walls. He was sitting on the same bench, in a clean, loose-fitting white shirt and immaculate white pants, in his straw hat and with a Bali hanging from his lower lip. He was looking straight ahead, as was his habit, and he seemed healthy. That noon, when we parted, he brusquely handed me some bills and said something about the trouble I'd gone to the day before. It was lots of money. I told him he didn't owe me anything, I would have done the same for any friend. The Grub insisted that I take the money. You can buy some books, he said. I have lots of books, I answered. This way you won't have to steal books for a few days, he said. At last, I accepted the money. A long time has gone by and I can't remember how much it was; the Mexican peso has lost value many times. I only remember that it was enough to buy twenty books and two records.

He never talked to me about Villaviciosa again. For a month and a half, maybe two months, we met each morning and parted at noon, when it was time for lunch and I went home on a city bus or a *pesero*. A few times, I invited him to the movies, but the Grub never wanted to go. He liked to talk to me as we sat in the Alameda or strolled the neighborhood, and sometimes he would deign to enter a bar, where he always sought out a turtle-egg vendor. I never saw him touch alcohol. A few days before he disappeared forever, he got it into his head to make me talk about Jacqueline Andere. I realized it was his way of remembering her. I talked about her ash-blond hair and compared it favorably or unfavorably to her honey-blond hair in the movies and the Grub nodded slightly, staring straight ahead, as if seeing her for the first time. Once I asked him what kind of women he liked. It was a stupid question from a kid just trying to pass the time. But the Grub took it literally and for a long time he pondered his response. At last he said: quiet women. And then he added: but only the dead are quiet. And after a while: not even the dead, when you think about it.

One morning he gave me a knife. The word *Caborca* was traced in silver on the bone handle. I remember that I thanked him effusively, and that morning, as we were talking in the Alameda or walking the crowded streets, I opened and shut it, admiring the grip, testing its weight in my hand, marveling at its perfect proportions, and frightening some passersby, who stepped away when they saw the knife, assuming an intent to harm that I by no means harbored. Otherwise, it was the same as any other day. The next morning, the Grub was gone.

Two days later, I went looking for him at his boarding-house and I was told that he had gone north. I never saw him again.

The Trip

Dora Montes boarded the *Donizetti* with approximately twenty other passengers, myself among them. The name of the port where we embarked sounded like a joke or gibberish. And maybe it really was gibberish, but it wasn't a joke in the Spanish sense of the term.

Then came the passage through the locks, with the passengers getting up early so as not to miss a thing (I slept in). And then, during breakfast, I saw her. She was sharing the table next to mine with her secretary, a brusque woman with very long straight hair who always wore black; a Peruvian businessman; and my cabinmate. I, in turn, was sitting with a Spanish Jesuit on his way to Bolivia, who would leave us in El Callao; a Chilean student returning from Europe; and the student's German wife, who was learning Spanish. I don't know whose idea it was to put us together. It had nothing to do with where we were from, or where our names fell in the alphabet, or whether our cabins were in the same section. It was just chance, and by lunchtime we discovered that the four of us at my table and the four at the neighboring table got along tolerably well, separately and even together, and any arguments would be civilized and easily settled.

My cabinmate was named Johnny Paredes and his parents were sending him to Chile to get him away from bad influences in Caracas. He talked like a Venezuelan and acted like a Venezuelan, but he was a Chilean who had been living there (where his parents had business interests) since he was two or three. He bragged about money. He was going to live with an aunt in Viña del Mar and he planned to hit the books and not make any male friends. The cabin had four berths, but it was just the two of us sharing it, and from the moment we met he made it clear to me that he wasn't a homosexual and that if I had any weird ideas I should forget them. We were the same age, but I looked older because of my long hair, mustache, and beard. It was the first time that Johnny Paredes had traveled alone and it showed. It was my first time too, but I hid it better because I'd been on the road for two months. Sometimes I remembered my parents saying goodbye to me at a Mexico City bus station and I felt sad and homesick. The neon sign on the station read Gran Estación del Sur, and it was the departure point for all travelers on their way to Puebla, Oaxaca, or Chiapas, and also for those heading to Guatemala. Like Johnny Paredes, I should have been in college, in my case at the Universidad Nacional Autónoma de México, but I had already been expelled from two high schools and my college future was as bleak as a hopeless old bolero. One night, my father told me I had a choice. I had to get a job, either in Mexico City or Sonora. I told him I'd rather go to Sonora. I was there for three months. One night, drunk and high, I visited my grandfather's grave in Santa Teresa, and the next morning I took the first bus back to Mexico City. I remember I felt terrible and I told the driver I would probably throw up along the way and the driver handed me a plastic bag and said not to worry. I also asked him to let me know when we passed through Villaviciosa, and then the driver looked at me with new eyes, as if he'd just realized that he had a madman on board, and he said the bus didn't go that way, but he would let me know when we were nearby, though all I'd see would be mountains. I said all right and then I fell asleep. When I woke up, I didn't know where I was. The sun was a blinding whitish yellow. To the left, said the driver. I looked, shading my eyes with my hand: all I saw were mountains, as he had said, and at the top of the mountains some unidentifiable trees, just a few of them, bare and dark with sparse branches. When I got home, I told my father that I had quit my job in Sonora. It wasn't right for me, I said. What do you want to do, then? asked my father. Join the revolution, I said. What revolution? asked my father. The American revolution, of course, I said. What American revolution? he asked. My mother, who had been silent up until now, said, Oh my God. Then I told them I was going back to Chile. The Chilean revolution? said my father. I nodded. But you're Mexican, said my father. No, I'm Chilean, I said, but it doesn't matter, all

Latin Americans should be on their way to Chile to support the revolution. Who's going to pay for your trip? asked my father. You, if you want to, I said, otherwise I'll hitch rides. That night, according to my sister, my father and mother cried for a long time, she heard them from her room. They must have been fucking, I said (I wish they had been). A week later, they gave me money to take a bus across Central America, and right there in Mexico City they bought me the ticket that would take me by ship from Panama to Valparaiso. Of course, they wanted me to fly, but I managed to convince them that traveling by land was formative, educational, and also cheaper. The idea of setting foot in an airport made my hair stand on end.

One afternoon, as I was writing, Dora Montes sat down next to me and struck up a conversation. She asked whether I was writing to my parents, then she asked if it was a letter to my girlfriend, and finally she wanted to know whether it was a diary. I said it wasn't a letter, I had no girlfriend, and I didn't keep a diary either. Surprisingly, once we had gotten to this point, Dora Montes's curiosity evaporated (I informed her later, unasked, that it was a story I was writing) and she began to tell me what she'd felt when we saw two whales from the deck that morning. She talked about mystical husbands, about life at sea, and finally about money, for some reason. It was that afternoon that she explained to me what she did for a living. She was a cabaret star. A stripper, to be precise. Now she was on her way back to Chile after a tour of sundry Central American night-clubs, all shady except for the Carrusel in Panama, where she had worked for two months. She would rather work in Santiago or Valparaiso, of course, but in Chile, she confessed, times were hard for burlesque artists. After six months, when her contract in Santiago expired, she would have to go back to Central America, and she was already depressed about it. She held out hope that her agent could book her some shows in Buenos Aires, though she humbly admitted that the competition there was strong.

Dora Montes must have been about thirty and she was dark haired, of average height, and fairly respectable. She saw the positive side of everything, though she didn't get excited about much. Her secretary (who was actually her sister, but I didn't know that until the second day of the trip) spent most of the day in bed on the poop deck, laid up by migraines that she believed were triggered by the sea air. At first glance, she seemed useless as a secretary or assistant and Johnny Paredes asked me a few times why the hell she was there. She was probably more useful behind the scenes on dry land, as a seamstress, treasurer, or nurse, than on a ship during a quiet sea crossing. As the days went by, I realized that Dora Montes would have killed herself if it hadn't been for the constant reassurance of her sister's subtle presence. In some mysterious way, Dora believed that her sister absorbed all of the ills that beset Dora herself (numerous ills, so she believed), meaning that if she drank too much, for example, it was her secretary who felt sick the next day. When I expressed my doubts about this strange link, Dora Montes claimed that it was a family trait and that her mother and her mother's older sister had the same connection. One night, when I got back from the dance hall, I found Dora and Johnny in bed together in our cabin. The next day, as I was writing, Dora came over and told me not to get the wrong idea about her. I said, Of course not, don't worry. Then she sat down next to me and, after a prolonged silence in which she gazed out to sea, then at my notebook, then back out to sea again, she proceeded to explain plainly and simply that it was all my fault. I remember that she was wearing light-blue bell-bottoms and her hair was gathered on her neck. It was very black hair, inky black, coarse to the touch. I don't know why, but all of a sudden I felt like hurting her. I told her that if she wanted to confess, we had a Spanish Jesuit on board. That was all. I regretted it almost immediately. But first, I felt Dora Montes fix me with a stare of disgust (I may even have enjoyed it). Then she got up, murmuring an insulting phrase as if to herself. This chilled me (it was the first time I'd heard such words on a woman's lips: filthy, unerring words, words that couldn't fail to hit their target), and in no way did I believe it was deserved. When I got back to my cabin that night, Johnny Paredes once again asked me to beat it to the deck for an hour.

Every night, the second-class passengers partied. There was a group that washed dishes in the kitchen by day and played for our dances by night. They were all Italians, and many of them were Communists who sympathized with the Chilean turn toward socialism. Sometimes they asked for a volunteer from the audience to come up onstage to sing or do magic tricks or tell jokes. When we came into port, they disappeared en masse and spent every minute they could at some brothel. Back on board the first night after we set out to sea again, they were so exhausted that they couldn't perform and we had to settle for music from a record player. The rest of the crew were calmer about shore calls and many didn't even disembark in port. The passengers bade farewell to those leaving the ship for good by waving handkerchiefs from the gangway, though moments later many of them also went ashore for a brief touristic visit. When I asked a Peruvian woman returning from Italy why the departing passengers' friends didn't say their goodbyes on dry land, her reply was that it was more romantic this way.

Sometimes we talked politics. At my table, the student returning from Europe declared himself a Christian Democrat. His German wife said that she was a Democrat, and the Spanish Jesuit claimed to be a leftist, broadly speaking, not specifying any particular party. At the neighboring table, Dora Montes said she wasn't interested in politics, while her sister confessed her sympathies lay on the right, and Johnny Paredes claimed to be resolutely apolitical (going so far as to idiotically declare: "After extensive study of the scene, I've chosen to opt out"). The Peruvian businessman, who was transporting pipes and tools bought secondhand in Panama and who was obsessed with Peruvian customs procedures, which he was constantly plotting to get around—he planned to pass off his cargo as personal baggage—murmured that he leaned slightly toward APRA, the indigenist party. The person I spent the most time talking to was the Jesuit. One night, leaning on the railing with Rita Pavone songs playing behind us, he lectured me on Erasmus and Spinoza's thinking as it related to the Latin American liberation struggles. In gratitude, I made him read my best story, about an extraterrestrial invasion. The extraterrestrials are a lot like ants: small, strong, organized, but more technologically advanced than man. The first spaceships to reach Earth (there are three of them) measure five feet long, one foot tall, and eighteen inches wide. At first, their intentions are peaceful. Talks are held with the United Nations, the ants are welcomed, and the ant ships remain in orbit around the planet, with the occasional mysterious foray over some small town, remote crossroads, or mountain range that no one has ever heard of. But after ninety days, when the hopes and expectations aroused by their presence are beginning to wane, two of the ships abandon their orbit in the stratosphere and land on a plantation in Jefferson County, West Virginia. It's a tobacco plantation, and it belongs to John Taeger. The county sheriff is alerted by the frightened landowner, and soon the plantation is overrun by state and federal authorities, policemen, soldiers from the Pentagon, television cameras, rubberneckers, etcetera. The extraterrestrial ants emerge from their ships in small flying contraptions no more than two inches in diameter and they open rudimentary channels of communication with the North American authorities. Meanwhile, other ants have begun to bore holes and raise towers constructed of something like fine, crisscrossing wire. After five hours, the Earth authorities decipher the message: the ants have decided to take possession of the place. The president of the United States, the UN Security Council, the world's top ufologists, and the higher-ups at the Pentagon are informed, but in the end no agreement is reached. The Taeger family is simply advised to abandon their house, and the plantation is surrounded by a strong security barrier. That night, of course, no one sleeps: not the agents controlling access to the plantation, not the national radar defense systems, not the reporters waiting for any news at the scene, not the sandwich and T-shirt vendors who've arrived at the plantation, and not John Taeger, who has roundly refused to leave his house and spends the night sitting on his porch, sometimes weeping bitterly, other times trying to find the positive side of this new and unexpected situation. The president of the United States calls the Soviet prime minister twice. The Soviet prime minister calls the American president once. The ants, surveilled with infrared equipment by the military police and the FBI, work all night. The next morning, the explosive news mysteriously appears in the papers. Not only do the extraterrestrial ants plan to uproot the Taeger family, they've laid claim to all of Jefferson County. The news, rapidly picked up by newspapers and TV channels all over the world, provokes contradictory reactions. At first, American public opinion is divided: there are those who refuse to relinquish a single square foot of sovereign soil and those who see the plans of the extraterrestrial insects as an opportunity for technological exchange; cooperation in the space race (with the ants' help, they'll show the Russians a thing or two); accelerated progress in astronomy, physics, astrophysics, and quantum mathematics—all in exchange for a fairly poor, rural county wholly devoted to the monoculture of a low-grade strain of tobacco. The next day, poor John Taeger suffers a heart attack, and meanwhile all kinds of meetings take place. The talks follow one after the other at a feverish pace. The Jefferson County Rotary Club proposes that the ants be deeded a similar piece of land in Honduras. The European and Warsaw Pact ambassadors trust that the American president will keep his head and try to bring matters to a peaceful conclusion. The experts make calculations: if there are five to ten thousand ants in the two ships that have landed on Taeger's farm, and if the ants are capable of reproducing on Earth, and if they have the power to eliminate their natural enemies, and if their lives are double or even triple as long as those of native Hymenoptera or Neuroptera, and if what they seek is found in abundance in Jefferson County (everything seems to indicate that this is so), it will be at least one hundred years before they demand to be granted another county with similar characteristics. Still, the voices of the warmongers grow louder on that first day of deliberations: a massive attack on the Taeger plantation, by air and by land, could wipe out the extraterrestrials in a single strike; a deal could be struck with the ship that is still orbiting the Earth, negotiated from a position of strength, or an agreement could be reached later, or the ship could be shot down; any other solution will only make the ants stronger, causing the extraterrestrial cancer to spread in the United States and ultimately all over the world. The day ends in exhaustion and expectation. The ants, per observers' reports, haven't stopped working for an instant. The next day, the president of the United States reaches a decision. The extraterrestrials are informed that the land they've claimed is the private property of John Taeger, who has no intention of selling it at this moment. In addition, whether for sale or not, his lands lie under the jurisdiction and flag of the United States of America; and therefore the ants must immediately cease their extraterrestrial excavations and/or construction, under the sun or underground, in Jefferson County, and immediately send a delegation to the White House to discuss the terms of their projected stay in the United States and on Earth in general. The ants' response is curt: they haven't come to despoil anyone, their intentions are essentially commercial and peaceful, they've chosen a rather small and not very populous county—basically, they don't think it's a big deal. Subsequent demands receive no response. The soldiers believe it's their turn to act. They plan to attack with overwhelming force, though on a limited scale, dropping bombs within a one-mile radius of the point where the two spaceships are still perched. The extraterrestrials maintain their silence, which some advisers interpret as indifference or even arrogance. After a full day of hesitation, the president gives the order to bomb. The area around Taeger's house and two other farms is evacuated, along with a crossroads made famous back in the day by a Colonel Mosby (his actions are commemorated on a moldy plaque that no one thinks to rescue), and the bombing gets underway. Planes drop a considerable quantity of bombs that have been successfully tested in Vietnam. But everything goes wrong. The few bombs that actually fall are neutralized by what a few science fiction writers, guests on live TV, describe with undisguised glee as a *magnetic force field* or an *electromagnetic protective barrier*. And most of the planes are shot down by a mysterious ray from the sky, soon identified by experts as issuing from the ship still in orbit around the Earth. But the ants' response is not simply to repel the attack. The ship's death ray—as it is dubbed by the tabloids—is immediately trained with hair-raising precision on the White House, reducing it to ashes. All of those present in the building are killed in the attack, including the president of the United States (Richard Nixon) and most of his advisers. The vice president (Spiro Agnew) takes over, putting Strategic Air Command on maximum alert, though minutes after being sworn in he's dissuaded by his own staff and others from launching a nuclear attack on West Virginia. A ground skirmish, led by the West Virginia National Guard and a commando unit specializing in biological and chemical warfare, ends in disaster, with the soldiers charred to the bone. After the storm, there is calm at last. The new American president suspends all preparations for war. The perimeter of the Taeger plantation, surrounded by security forces, is abandoned. The troops that could previously be seen moving through some Jefferson County towns vanish. As the weeks go by, the de facto sovereignty of the ants—or at least their free usufruct of Jefferson County—is established. Many of its inhabitants abandon their homes and move to California. Others wait to see what will happen. But nothing happens; they're able to remain in their houses, they're able to drive the roads unhampered by ant checkpoints, they're able to leave the county and return without being bothered. In fact, very few people have seen the extraterrestrial ants at all, and in some newspapers in Idaho and Montana (and several Latin American papers) voices question whether the ants really exist. For those who live close to the old Taeger plantation, however, things have changed: no one dares to step on an ant, let alone an anthill; in summer, insecticide is used only inside, on the assumption that the extraterrestrials would never fall into such an obvious trap. All over the world, especially among writers and artists, cases of zoopsia are up 1,000 percent. Some attribute this to a rise in alcoholism and drug use. Others, more diplomatic, see it as a case of sensitive souls responding to a future threat. One day, every radar system on Earth registers the takeoff of the two ships remaining in Jefferson County. Shortly afterward, before anyone can really believe it, the news spreads all over the world. Of the three ant ships, one is still in orbit around the Earth and the other two have disappeared into the vastness of space, probably on their way back to their home planet. On the old Taeger plantation, according to spy plane photographs and the occasional bold interloper, things have scarcely changed: there are five braided-wire towers scarcely five feet tall, spaced sixteen inches apart, with the small wasp ships hovering around them every so often. The rest of the colony is clearly underground. No one in Jefferson County has yet made physical contact with the extraterrestrials. In view of this new situation, the Pentagon proposes another attack. The president hesitates or pretends to hesitate. He consults with friendly powers, who advise him to talk to the Russians, but the president and his staff believe that the Soviets are capable of disclosing their plans to the ants. The president has many considerations to weigh, but ultimately it's the vision of the White House and its nuclear-proof underground bunker in ruins that prevails. To the relief of many, a détente is reached. A new era begins on Earth. The United Nations offers the ants a seat in the permanent assembly, a seat that they reject for the sake of decorum. Despite everything, fluid communications are established between Earth dwellers and extraterrestrials. A group of experts who have gathered along the property line of the old Taeger plantation, where they set up their machinery and tents, state that it will be at least fifty years before the extraterrestrials outgrow Jefferson County, since it's been two months and they have yet to reach the house's backyard. As time goes by, greater knowledge of the ants will make them more accessible and therefore more vulnerable. Papers are pub-lished and a few conclusions are reached: the ants subsist on a different diet than their sisters on Earth; everything seems to indicate that they possess no written language; their culture is oneiric; the land on which they've settled hasn't undergone noticeable surface changes. All of these conclusions are partial, of course. According to the local farmers, the ants eat ants. A tour guide at the Great Pyramid in Teotihuacán says that he's seen extraterrestrial ships no bigger than a pack of cigarettes hovering near the many anthills around the pyramid. The Earth ants are led one by one into the spaceships. A missionary priest in the Amazon claims to have witnessed an epiphany (God forgive me) above a swarm of red ants in the region of Manicoré. According to the missionary, the red ants were raised silently into flying objects that looked a lot like black boiled eggs, riddled with cracks. Around the nest, the red ants clambered over one another instead of fleeing, as if trying to touch their antennas to the eggs that . . .

The story was unfinished. I might expand it and turn it into a novel, I said to the Jesuit. The Jesuit said nothing. Maybe he hadn't liked the last part, about the Amazon missionary. When I got back to the party, I thought about making some changes and asking him to read it again. But then Dora Montes's secretary came in and I forgot about the story and the Jesuit. Dora is about to do something desperate, was the first thing she said. I was sitting and she was leaning over me, speaking almost into my ear. She smelled spicy, a combination of Italian food and perfume. I asked what she meant. Why would Dora do something desperate? For love, why else, said the secretary, sitting down next to me. Her hand felt for mine under the table and she furtively handed me a bill. Buy me a drink, she said, smiling. When I got up, I tried to see whether Dora Montes had come into the room, but I couldn't spot her. When I came back with two whiskeys, I handed the secretary the change over the table and I asked her to explain clearly to me what was wrong with Dora. She's going to strip in front of everyone, she said, fixing me with her gaze. And it's your fault, she added.

One of the most indelible memories of my return trip to Chile is a night that I spent at a boardinghouse in Guatemala. The walls were probably thin and the head of my bed must have been against the head of the bed in the neighboring room. At first everything was silent and I settled down to finish a book while having a peaceful smoke. The book was Pierre Louÿs's *Aphrodite*. At some point I must have fallen asleep. Then I heard voices and I woke up. It was two men talking. By their accents I could tell that they weren't Mexican. One of them might have been Central American; the other, Venezuelan or Panamanian. I don't know why, but I imagined that the second man was black. Their room had two beds, like my room, and the Central American was in the bed up against mine: for a moment I imagined his head resting on the exact same piece of wall as mine. Even before I woke up, I knew what they were talking or arguing about: that's the only way I can explain the distress I felt. The Central American was talking about knives. The Venezuelan, who might have been even more upset than I, was expounding on different brands of knives. The Central American told him to shut up, saying all that mattered was the arm that wielded the knife. The Venezuelan expounded on famous Venezuelan knife fighters. The Central American said that all this (all what?) was sissy chatter, real fighters lived in anonymity. The Venezuelan agreed, saying that anonymity and humility were man's Sunday suit. The Central American said that men who wore Sunday suits didn't deserve to call themselves men. The Venezuelan assented, undeterred, and said that he was absolutely right, real men wore good suits every day of the week. The Central American said that real men lived in anonymity and blood, no suit required. Anonymity and blood, said the Venezuelan. That's poetry. Beautiful. The Central American coughed then, as if the presence of the Venezuelan was suffocating him, and he told a story. The story was about a woman, a showgirl like Dora Montes, whom he'd grown fond of. A beautiful woman, he said, twenty-eight but still in great shape, serious and hardworking. A woman with whom he had a son or a daughter (it wasn't clear; he might even have been referring to the woman's child from a previous lover) and with whom he lived happily for a while. A woman he put to work and who didn't complain. A woman he could curse at and hit, never hearing anything from her lips but the most reasonable complaints (he used the word *reasonable* several times and also *sense* and *nonsense*). So what happened, compadre? asked the Venezuelan in a quavering voice. I imagined him as black, maybe a boxer, stronger than the Central American in any case, capable of knocking him down nine times out of ten, but reluctant to fight, wanting to sleep and get back on the road the next day. What happened? asked the Central American, close to my ear. What happened to that happy life, compadre? repeated the Venezuelan. Five months ago, I killed her, said the Central American. And then: with a kitchen knife. And much later: I buried her in the yard of our little love nest. And finally, just as I was about to fall asleep: I said that she had gone on tour. That's what you told the authorities, compadre? The police, yes, said the Central American, in a voice tinged with sleep, weariness, even vulnerability, any drunkenness or aggression gone.

That night, I found Dora Montes on the forecastle deck, in an area reserved for the very few first-class passengers. She was drunk. I told her she was in no condition to strip, and I took her back to my cabin. We made love until Johnny Paredes came in. Dora, unlike many drunks whose bodies go limp or unsynchronized, was taut and moved with mathematical precision. Christ, said Johnny Paredes when he turned on the light, I've been looking for you for hours, your sister told me you wanted to kill yourself. Then he sat on his bunk and we all started to talk. According to Dora, she was just sad and she had no plans to kill herself (only fools did that), let alone take off her clothes in public. My sister must have made that up to get you to come after me, she said, looking me in the eyes. I can come back in an hour, if you want, said Johnny Paredes. No need, said Dora, get in your bunk and go to sleep. Johnny turned off the light and got undressed in the dark. Good night, he said. Good night, we said. It was too dark to see anything, but I knew that Dora was smiling.

The next afternoon Dora made love with Johnny Paredes. That night, she came back to make love with me, and when we reached Arica, to celebrate our arrival on Chilean terrain all three of us made love together, which was a disaster. Johnny and I kept watching each other surreptitiously and in the end Dora burst out laughing.

We reached Valparaiso at night and for reasons unknown they wouldn't let us disembark until the next morning. That night, Dora Montes, her secretary, Johnny Paredes, and I stayed up late on deck talking, gazing at the lights in the mountains, and listening to Chilean radio. I remember that Johnny told stories about gang members in Caracas, probably made up; Dora and her sister told stories about Central American night-clubs; and I said that in Panama I had seen *Last Tango in Paris* and met a black waiter at the bar on the ground floor of my rooming house who had seen every single movie made in Mexico and who advised me not to go back to Chile. Dora and her sister didn't say anything. But Johnny seemed interested. Why did he tell you not to go back? I don't know, I said. He was black, skinny, and I think he was gay. He said he liked me. Oh, said Johnny, now I get it. He even told me he knew how to resell the boat ticket so I could go back to Mexico. Stop right there, said Johnny, it's plain as day.

The next day we left the ship. Johnny Paredes was met by his aunt from Viña del Mar. Dora and her secretary were met by two big men with mustaches and dark suits. Our goodbyes were formal. Then I shouldered my backpack and set off on foot for the train station.

4.

The Coup

I was dreaming about a woman with bright eyes when shouts woke me. It was Juan de la Cruz, a painter and sculptor of virgins, whose house I was staying in. My first thought was that I was being kicked out or that I had a phone call from Mexico, something serious to do with my mother's health, maybe. Then I realized that Juan de la Cruz was moaning, not shouting, and that he was tearing at his hair with one hand as he shook me by the shoulder with the other, though his voice barely rose above a whisper, as if he was afraid he would be overheard. I jumped out of bed naked and asked whether there was a call for me. The painter sat down on the bed that I had just abandoned and said not to worry, my mother was fine, or he guessed she was, and then he said that he wished he could be with my mother right now, or even my father, or begging for change around Chapultepec (which is something that makes an impression on tourists—Juan de la Cruz had been in Mexico not long ago). The military has risen up, he said, it's all over. My first feeling was relief. My mother was fine, my family was fine. I got dressed and went into the bathroom to wash my face and brush my teeth, followed by the painter, who summed up for me over and over again what had happened so far, and then we had a cup of tea together. I asked what he planned to do. What can I do? he said, I'm an artist, it's all over.

I didn't see it that way, and before I left I took my Caborca knife from my backpack and put it in my pocket. This was a working-class neighborhood of single-story houses with back and front yards, stretching endlessly along the highway south from Santiago. On the other side of the highway rose a new shantytown with narrow unpaved streets, linked to the neighborhood and its shops via a few very high pedestrian walkways. Along both sides of the highway were many vacant lots.

There was no one outside, but I knew that the painter's neighbors were Socialists because people came into their yards at night to talk and we'd spoken once. So I crossed the street and knocked on their door. I wasn't a Communist or a Socialist but it didn't seem like the kind of day to be choosy about your comrades. The Socialists were orphans. One was seventeen and the other was fifteen and they were having breakfast when I got there. They lived with an older brother, who was twenty and who had left for the factory a while ago. They offered me a cup of tea and at first I got the impression that their brother had gone to work. Then I realized that he hadn't, that nobody was going to work that day.

One of the Socialists said that the local Communist cell was handing out weapons and coordinating the actions of all the leftist groups, and after we finished our tea we went there. The cell's headquarters were at the house of an ordinary working-man, a fat little guy who was clearly rattled by the presence of so many strangers in his dining room. At times he seemed about to cry, though at the critical moment he always pulled himself together. The Socialist brothers had been there before, and they introduced me succinctly: a comrade, they said, and the fat man and his wife said good morning, comrade, shrugging their shoulders.

Every new arrival brought fresh and contradictory reports. They talked all at once and the fat man sometimes took refuge in a corner under the portrait of a man and a woman, also fat and smiling literally from ear to ear, who must have been his parents, and then he would pull a handful of coins out of his pocket, count them, and put them back again. Following this, he would sink his head in his hands and try to think.

There were more than fifteen of us congregated in the dining room and we represented nearly the full spectrum of the Chilean left, official and clandestine. The fat man's wife came out of the kitchen with a tray full of glasses and a teapot. Suddenly the noise level dropped and we all sat down wherever we could, mostly on the floor, and drank tea. I remember that we called each other *comrade*, even though we'd hardly met before today. Among the young people, especially, the camaraderie was intense. As soon as things were quiet, the fat man said that we should contact the organization to get concrete orders and trustworthy information. This mission, which had to be carried out in broad daylight, under curfew, and on a bicycle, was assigned to me. Then I realized that they all thought I was a foreigner (and therefore a seasoned activist) and I hurried to correct the misunderstanding. I told them that I was Chilean, that I had a different accent because I had just arrived from Mexico where I had been living for years, that I had no experience in situations like this, and I hardly knew Santiago. The news plunged all of them—but especially the fat man—into deep gloom. For a second I thought he was about to tell us to go home. But he clung to his plan and asked for a volunteer. Everyone turned him down for one reason or another. The fat man's wife gazed at us sadly from the kitchen. All right, said the fat man, settling the matter, I'll go myself.

Some of us went outside to see him off or to advise him on the best route. Avoiding the busiest streets, it would take him twenty minutes at least. Before he left, the fat man said good-bye to his children and then he got on his bicycle and rode off. He was the only person out on those empty streets and he struggled to keep his balance. As far as I know, he never came home again.

Then the fat man's wife made more tea and we poured another round. Some people started to talk about soccer. The crowd broke up into pairs and threesomes. One group was telling jokes. The walls and the floor were wooden and they smelled nice. Suddenly I felt tired and I could easily have gone to sleep. The fat man seemed to have taken the dream of History with him, and deep down, those of us left at the house knew—some of us more definitely, other less so—that it was all over.

After a while another Communist turned up, a guy in a sweater that looked like it was knit out of hair, and he said it was an outrage to see so many people sitting around with nothing better to do than drink tea. It's about time you got here, Pancho, said the fat man's wife. We gathered that this Pancho was the cell boss and the fat man had filled in for him in his absence. The Socialist brothers and some of the younger guys, all in their teens, said that they were looking for action, but since there were no guns we were making do with tea. You'll get action, said Pancho, and he sat at the head of the table and made us line up. He wrote down our names on a piece of paper, and then the streets that we should guard, and finally our code names. What name do you want? he asked me when it was my turn. I wanted Ernesto but somebody had already claimed it, so I said the first name that came into my head: Enrique. Then Pancho gave us the password: Looks like it's going to rain, we had to say when anybody approached us (probably Pancho himself, but it might also be another comrade) and he would reply, It's a cold morning. Then we had to say, Could be worse, which meant that there had been no movement of right-wing radicals on the street, or, It's going to rain cats and dogs, which meant the exact opposite. I was assigned to guard a street near where I lived. When I asked what right-wing radicals I should be watching out for, nobody knew what to tell me. Then we left one by one on our respective missions.

Those were the worst two hours of my life, hours spent sitting in the street where there wasn't a soul to be seen, staring at shuttered houses. I knew that I was being watched too, and I could understand why people would be curious. Frankly, they were right to keep an eye on me: only a crazy person would sit in the middle of an empty street, in deep contemplation of nothingness, risking arrest if an army jeep drove by. Once, I saw some kids watching me from a window. Another time, a woman came into the yard with her dog (the dog wanted to go out, but the woman held him back and we talked for a while). Otherwise, there was no movement at the house or houses of the supposed right-wingers, and why should there be? The work was being done by others—and done impeccably, to judge by the planes that from time to time I saw, as if in a dream, pass above from one cloud to another.

When at last I saw Pancho approaching, all I cared about was getting out of there. He wasn't alone. A tall young guy with wet hair, as if freshly washed, was with him. It's a cold morning, Pancho said. Suddenly I realized that I didn't remember the password, and I said so. I can't remember the password, comrade, but everything's quiet here (in fact, our presence on the street was the only deviation from the new normal). What are we doing standing here? I wondered. Pancho looked at me as if he didn't know me and he feared an ambush or worse. His companion—I could tell by the expression on his face when he heard my excuse—was ready to beat me up on the spot. The cell boss tried again: It's a cold morning. This time I decided to ignore him and give him a brief report of everything that had happened in the past two hours: there's been no movement of right-wing elements, I said, my sense is that people are scared, I haven't seen any military patrols, a woman who came out with her dog told me that they're bombing La Moneda. It's a cold morning, Pancho repeated. I don't know why, but at that moment I felt a kind of affection for him, for the thug with him, and for myself, not having brought a single book to while away the long wait.

One of the two of us had to admit defeat, but neither Pancho nor I was willing. Asking, answering; utterly lost to each other.

FRENCH

COMEDY

OF

HORRORS

For Lautaro and Alexandra Bolaño

That day, if I'm not mistaken, was the day of the eclipse. We, the friends of Roger Bolamba, had settled down at the House of the Sun, a soda fountain that is, or was, at the curve of the seaside promenade along the stretch officially known as avenue Colonel Goffin. As we waited for the spectacle of the eclipse, we talked about poetry and politics, which was what we always talked about anyway. We had chosen a table next to the window overlooking the cliff, which wasn't the best seat in the house, but it wasn't bad either. Though it was true that the waiters hardly paid any attention to us and served us last, Bolamba presided over the table with his usual dignity and we— who were young and inexperienced back then—felt like princes.

Next to our table was a guy in a white cotton blazer, black shirt, and bloodred tie. He was big, six feet tall at least, and he was drinking rum with Guyanita-Cola. With him were two women. One was older, and she was looking all around, as if the festive atmosphere at the House of the Sun scared her. The other was much younger, and every so often she cuddled up to the well-dressed guy, whispering words that I couldn't quite make out.

I remember the guy because when the eclipse started he got up from his table and started to dance, staring straight at the sun (the rest of us were all looking at it through film negatives or special sunglasses, and some of us even had bits of dark glass, probably pieces of beer bottles), and after a few seconds the older woman joined him in a kind of *chacona* or *resbalosa*, a *galleada* maybe or a *sombrilla*, a dance that was somehow anachronistic but at the same time terrifying, and that, according to Bolamba, was known only deep in the northern rain forests, in other words the poorest and most remote parts of the country, the malarial forests, the half-abandoned villages near the border where dengue and superstition ruled.

But that wasn't all. On the one hand, the sun was gradually dimming until it went completely black. On the other hand, the well-dressed guy and the older woman were dancing a *sombrilla*, which sometimes seemed more like a *resbalosa*, or a *chacona* (because of the precision of the steps), or a *galleada* (because of the obscene moves), singing softly and watching the solar show without blinking. They looked like two people possessed, not in a violent way, but in a resigned, bureaucratic way. The girl, oblivious to the eclipse, had eyes only for them, as if their highly predictable spins were the most interesting thing happening. I should also say that of all the people pressing their noses to the glass at the House of the Sun, it's possible (though I may be presuming too much) that, other than the girl, I was the only one watching what was happening inside as well as out. When the eclipse was over, we all—those of us in Roger Bolamba's circle, that is—held our breath and clapped. The other patrons followed our lead and the applause was universal and thunderous. Even the well-dressed guy stopped dancing and bowed with a flourish, submissive and sardonic. Just then the older woman cried out.

"I've gone blind!" she shouted.

The waiters at the House of the Sun, who were watching the sky from behind tinted glasses, looked at her and laughed. The well-dressed guy patted the air, searching for the body of the older woman, who had sat down on the floor. The girl got up from the table and took him by the hand.

"The eclipse is over," she said. "Now we can go, love."

With a jab of my elbow, I alerted my friend David Alan to what was happening behind his back, but after glancing at the three people attracting my attention, he turned back to the otherworldly darkness blowing over the streets and hills of Port Hope. Then the girl helped the older woman up from the floor, calling her *mamá*, mother, life-giver, madam, *señora*, sainted lady, as tears spilled down her cheeks. What an absurd performance, I remember thinking. The well-dressed guy, sitting at the table again, wound a shiny wristwatch, which certainly didn't look cheap. I turned away. The sea below had suddenly grown calm and the tide, according to Roger Bolamba, didn't know whether to come in or go out. We heard a dog bark. Past the cliff, where the promenade runs along the beach, we saw a man walk into the water and then swim out to the buoy. The buildings on the waterfront seemed to have shifted, tilting slightly toward the south, like psychopathic Towers of Pisa. The few clouds plying the sky of Port Hope had disappeared. A sound like charcoal against dry wood, like stone against gem, imperceptibly scored the air of the capital. Roger Bolamba, who had been the one to invite us to the soda fountain, said that we would watch the next solar eclipse in bathing trunks on the beach, and then we would follow the example of the swimmer who was making his way toward the buoy.

"When is the next eclipse?" asked someone I didn't recognize.

"Thirty years from now," said David Alan.

When I turned to look at the well-dressed guy and the women with him, they were gone. Then the sun shone again through the windows and most of us pocketed the devices we had used to protect our eyes from the dangerous rays of the blazing orb (or tossed them on the floor), except for the waiters, who were still wearing their glasses at work five years later, starting a trend that was gradually picked up by hotel waiters, beach restaurant waiters, and finally dance club waiters.

The rest of the afternoon proceeded as usual: somebody wrote a sonnet to the eclipse; somebody compared the eclipse to the state of the arts in our country; somebody said that children conceived during an eclipse were born with birth defects or just flat-out evil, which meant that it wasn't a good idea to make love during an eclipse, total or partial. Then it was time to pay and we all dug into our pockets. As usual, somebody was out of cash, or didn't have enough, or hadn't brought cash with him, and among all of us, democratically, we had to cover what he'd ordered, a beer, a coffee, a dish of pineapple preserves. Nothing very expensive, as you can see, though when you're poor anything that isn't free is expensive.

Later, the owner of the soda fountain—who respected Bolamba's past as an athlete and grudgingly accepted his new literary calling—ordered us to leave, which we did willingly, since there was no air conditioning at the House of the Sun and by then the heat had become unbearable. Our conversation continued at De Gaulle Park, the biggest park in the city, where we sprawled on the green grass that no one had cut for more than a month, as Alcides La Mouette pointed out, because of the strike of city contractors, which included gardeners and caretakers, but not garbagemen, whose work regulations were different. So the grass was taller than usual (much taller) and we lay down in it, Roger Bolamba and the five or six of us who followed him everywhere, as the pot and amphetamine dealers settled on the cement or stone benches that had replaced the original cast-iron benches, which someone had stolen and sold to the rich and cultivated families of our city.

As always, we read aloud the news published in the literary section of the *Port Hope Monitor*, dreary news, the names of academics who had gone on to better places, the names of others who were still swarming the basements of the Ministry of External Affairs or the Ministry of Health and Social Welfare, occupied with complex heuristic challenges. Alongside them, shining bright, were the young people (though some of these young people were past fifty) who would replace them, though for the moment they spent their time writing about the flora and fauna of our republic. It was they whom Roger Bolamba most hated or envied, because they were of his generation and they were, to a certain extent, those directly responsible for his marginal position in national literary circles. As always, we laughed at their poems, we laughed at their translations (there was one of a German writer that made him sound like a stuttering Creole), we laughed at their reviews, dithyrambic in most cases, affected paeans to the masters with nods to colleagues or friends. Then the sun began to set and a breeze blew from the south and we all went with Bolamba to his house, which was by the port, a little fisherman's house, where books jostled for space with the cups and medals that our mentor had won over the course of his long athletic career.

There, as usual, he poured us each a shot of rum, which we downed in a single gulp, and then, also as usual, we piled our hands over Bolamba's outstretched hands and shouted:

"To victory!"

Then we left and let our teacher rest.

But that night, a kind of melancholy shone weakly in my comrades' eyes, as if the Bolambaesque cheer wasn't enough, or as if we were getting older. Alcides La Mouette put it plainly.

"Where will we be fifteen years from now? Where will we be thirty years from now, when the next eclipse comes to Port Hope? We'll be working in pharmacies, as clerks, or we'll have left for the provinces to lead miserable lives. We'll have children and aches and pains. No one will write. And this shit country will be just the same as it is now."

"Not the same," said David Alan. "Probably worse. Much worse, even."

"Then we won't be alive," I said, "because if the country gets any worse we'll have no choice but to head for the rain forest."

"Maybe so," said David Alan.

We had reached the center of the city and the neon signs shaded my friends' faces yellow, then blue, then red. We shook hands formally and parted ways. I started for the Coves, which was where my mother had a stand selling fried fish, yucca, and beans. Alan and La Mouette headed to New Town, which was a workers' housing complex that a Belgian architect had built ten years ago on the edge of the city, next to two mills; it was already falling down. As I walked, I started to whistle a popular song. Then I passed some white kids, who must have been tourists though they didn't look like it, and I composed a poem in my head about human solidarity, more powerful than race or nationality. The white kids, one girl among them, got into a Cadillac convertible and peeled off, making the tires squeal. I stood there watching the trail of exhaust they left until they disappeared down avenue de l'Indépendance. When I got to the stop, my bus was long gone and I decided to save the money and walk.

I don't know why, but I resolved to take a shortcut (or what I thought was a shortcut) through the hills. I had never gone that way before. Whenever I was on foot, I walked along rue du Commerce, where the thronging masses were up and about until late. Maybe that particular night I wasn't in the mood for thronging masses; maybe I wanted to try a new route; maybe I wanted to breathe the fresher air of the upper reaches of Port Hope.

All I know for sure is that instead of turning right toward the sea, I turned left onto a fairly wide street running uphill, almost imperceptibly at first. I can't remember what it was called. After a while, the palm trees to either side of the street vanished, replaced by pines, big royal pines that towered in the night. The sounds of the city vanished too and all that was left was the muted rumble of a few cars and the chorus of night birds calling to one another. I recognized the heehee bird, which seems to be laughing at everyone, and I thought I also made out the call of the radiator bird, whose song or cry is full of ennui.

Then I passed a gas station that still had all its lights on but where I didn't see a single person. I noticed this immediately and was a little alarmed, since in those days gas station robberies were a common occurrence, according to the papers. I walked faster and, when I had left the gas station behind, I realized that the road was getting steeper and there were fences on either side now instead of houses, as if the land had only just been parceled out. Each lot had a different fence. The side streets weren't paved.

When I got to the top of the hill I saw the sea and the lights of the port and the traffic along the promenade. I didn't see the lights of the Coves, which was on the other side of the bay, on the banks of the Coconut River. For a second, I thought that my sense of direction had abandoned me. But I was sure that if I kept walking and got over the second hill I'd soon be in the Old Hospital neighborhood, which I knew like the palm of my hand, and from there it was steps to the beach.

So I kept walking until I reached a lush plaza, full of trees and big dark plants that made strange sounds in the breeze. As if they were talking. As if they were all mulling over the same story. As if the eclipse, which wouldn't come again for another thirty years, had settled permanently in their leaves. And I heard the heehee bird again. It was calling to another bird, or so I guessed, but there was no answer. Hee hee, hee hee, hee hee, from the top of a pine. And then the silent wait. No answer. Then the bird called again and waited again, and again the same result. It was still in good humor despite the fruitlessness of its call, I mused. It must be laughing at itself, not at anyone listening to it. Then, without thinking, I answered it.

"Hee hee," I said, under my breath at first, like a shy heehee bird, then louder, until I hit the right pitch.

The silence that fell suddenly over the plaza gave me goose

bumps. It wasn't just that the heehee bird didn't answer, it was as if all the plants were turning to look at me. Feeling watched didn't discourage me and I called to the bird again in its own tongue, which consisted of just two syllables, meaning that any verbal nuance must come from the tone in which they were uttered. Maybe, I said to myself, the heehee bird's hee hee meant *I'm alone, I want a girl bird*, or *I'm ready and waiting, I want a girl bird*, and my answering hee hee might mean *I'm going to kill you, I'm going to rip you to pieces, I want your feathers*, say, or *I want your guts*.

As might have been expected, there was no answer. I imagined the heehee bird hidden on some branch, watching me with a sardonic smile on its beak, the smile of an old joker with the words *trickery* and *blood* hanging from it like worms. On the other side of the plaza, the street split in two. Mentally I asked the bird to forgive me for the joke I had just played on it and I turned down the street to the right, which was possibly better lit than the street on the left.

At first the street went downhill, but after a while it leveled off. The houses were big and each had a yard and a garage, though some late-model cars were parked along the curb. The street smelled like freshly watered plants. The grass in the yards looked neatly cut—unlike, say, the grass at De Gaulle Park. Every few feet there was a streetlight and, as if that weren't light enough, almost every house had a little porch lamp wreathed in mosquitoes and moths. Through a few windows, I caught glimpses of people up late talking, or watching the late shows on TV, though my general sense was that most of the street's residents were asleep already.

I walked faster. Across the street, next to a streetlight and an enormous pine, there was a telephone booth. I remember I thought it was strange, even ludicrous, to see a telephone booth in a neighborhood where everybody surely had phones at home. The public telephone nearest to us was more than three blocks away and most of the time it didn't work, so when my mother or I needed to make a phone call we had to walk at least six blocks to the next phone, which was on rue du Vélodrome, by the seafood stands. Just then, as I was walking along the opposite sidewalk, the phone rang.

I slowed down but didn't stop. I heard the first ring clearly, then the second. I imagined that a boy or a girl would come running across one of those verdant yards to answer it. The third ring sent a shiver through me, then came the fourth and the fifth and I stopped. For an instant, I thought that the noise would wake up the neighbors and they would see me walking down their street, a stranger whom they would probably take for a thief. The phone rang for the sixth time, then the seventh. I ran across the street. When I got to the other side, I stopped and imagined that it would stop ringing, but then came the eighth and the ninth ring, magnified. Before the phone could ring for the tenth time, I slid into the booth and picked up the receiver.

"Who is it?" asked a voice that didn't sound south Guianan or central Guianan, much less north Guianan.

"Me," I said, stupidly.

"Good, very good. What's your name?" The voice didn't have a French accent either. We were speaking in French, of course, but it didn't sound like the voice of someone from France. It might have been the voice of a Pole speaking French, say, or a Serb speaking French.

"Diodorus Pilon."

"Diodorus of Sicily? Nice name, very original," said the voice. "Wait a minute, I'm going to write it down." I heard a kind of laugh and I guessed it was a joke. "All right, Diodorus, you're young and you're a poet, am I right?"

"Yes."

"Tell me how old you are, if you don't mind."

"Seventeen."

"Do you have a book out yet? Have you published poems in a literary magazine? Newspapers, broadsheets, bulletins, literary supplements, church newsletters?"

"Actually, no. None of my poems have ever been published."

"Do you have a book in the works? Do you have plans to publish something—anything—soon?"

"No."

"Okay, okay. Wait a minute, Diodorus, don't hang up . . ."

I heard a crunch. As if someone had split a slender plank of wood with one blow. I heard static. Muffled curses and grumbling. Then silence. Outside of the booth, in the street, everything seemed normal. I imagined the neighbors and their children sleeping. I imagined kids who lived on that street I had never seen before. I saw them coming out in the morning on their way to school or college, dressed in miniskirts or prestigious uniforms. I thought about my mother, who was waiting for me at the Coves.

"Do you have any idea who I am, Diodorus?" asked the voice all of a sudden.

"No."

"Not the slightest idea?"

"Maybe this is a joke," I ventured.

"Not even close. This isn't a joke. You really don't have the slightest idea why we've called you?"

"You didn't actually call me. I was just passing by, and I happened to pick up the phone."

"No, Diodorus. We were calling you. We knew that if you were walking by a phone and it rang, you would answer it. We've called lots of public phones, of course. All of the phones on the four or five routes you might have taken tonight."

"This is the first time I've been on this street."

"It's called Elm Street. Though I don't think there are any elms on it."

"You're right, there are only pines."

"But it's a pretty street. Anyway. Let me ask you the same question again. Do you have any idea who we are?"

"No," I confessed.

"Would you like to know? Do you want to hear our proposal?"

"I'm dying to hear it," I said.

"We belong . . . No, 'belong' isn't the right word, because we don't belong to anyone or anything . . . We really only belong to ourselves. And sometimes, Diodorus, even that isn't certain. Do I sound a trifle moralistic?" he asked, after a moment of reflection.

"Not at all. I agree completely with everything you've said. Man belongs only to himself."

"Well, that's not quite it, but close. I think we've gotten a little off track."

"You were going to tell me the name of your organization," I said, helpfully.

"Oh yes. We're the Clandestine Surrealist Group."

"The Clandestine Surrealist Group."

"Or the Surrealist Group in Clandestinity. The CSG, for short."

"Do you belong to the CSG?" I shouted in excitement.

"Let's say that I serve in the CSG. Have you ever heard of us?"

"Honestly, no."

"Not many people have, Diodorus, that's part of our strategy. I know you've heard of surrealism, haven't you?"

"Of course. My mentor, Roger Bolamba, was a friend of the great south Guianan poet Régis Saint-Clair, about whom Breton said: 'His horse is the night.'"

"Is that true?"

"Absolutely."

"Wait a minute, Diodorus, don't hang up."

I heard a voice cursing in a language that definitely wasn't French. It had to be some Slavic or Balkan language.

"Régis Saint-Clair . . . Saint-Clair, Saint-Clair, Saint-Clair . . . I've got it. South Guianan poet, member of the surrealists from 1946 to 1950. Born at Shark Point, lived many years in Africa. Author of some twenty books celebrating negritude, Creole food, the mental landscape of exile . . . The mental landscape of exile—who wrote that, I'd like to know . . . At the end of his career he returns to south Guiana, where he's head of the National Library . . . Dies of natural causes at his Shark Point home. Is that the man?"

"Yes, sir. Régis Saint-Clair."

"And you say he was a friend of your mentor, what was his name, Bolamba?"

"Roger Bolamba. They were as close as dirt and fingernail. Pardon the expression."

"Bury your mentors, Diodorus. Now that you're seventeen, I'd say that the moment has come."

"I'll think about it, sir," I said, very excited for some reason.

"Now, where were we? You were saying that you're familiar with surrealism, is that right?"

"The best poets in the world," I said with conviction.

"Not just poets, Diodorus, painters and filmmakers too."

"I love Buñuel."

"But especially revolutionaries, Diodorus. Now listen up.

There are prophets, seers, sages, sorcerers, necromancers, mediums. But those are really only disguises. Sometimes good disguises and sometimes clumsy disguises. But disguises all the same, do you follow me?"

"I follow you," I said, uncertainly.

"And what do these disguises hide? They hide revolutionaries. Because that's what it's all about, do you see?"

"Yes," I said. "Revolutionaries hide to make revolution."

"No," said the voice. "The revolution is made without disguises. Revolutionaries hide to prepare for revolution."

"I understand."

"And broadly speaking, that's what the Clandestine Surrealist Group is. A surrealist group that nobody knows anything about. We need publicity," he said, and he started to laugh. He didn't laugh like a Frenchman but like a Pole or a Russian who has been living in Paris for a long time. "And that explains this sort-of proselytism, though that's not quite the right word for it, this sort-of selection process, shall we say, that we conduct through phone calls."

"So what about surrealism? The . . . official surrealism? Why doesn't it take charge of the selection process?" I asked.

"Official surrealism is a whorehouse, Diodorus. The stories I could tell you . . . Since Breton died, there's no enduring that crowd. Don't get me wrong. A few of them are good people, especially some of the widows, the surrealist widows tend to be exceptional people, but the vast majority are absolute twits.

If it were up to me I'd hang them all from the lampposts of the Champs-Elysées."

"I agree," I said.

"In fact," said the voice, dreamily, "official surrealism, the usual worthy exceptions aside, is unaware of the existence of the CSG. To give you an idea, imagine a flesh-and-blood person like you or me living in a room, and living in the same room—though I don't know whether 'living' is quite the word—is a ghost. Sharing the same scenery or surroundings. But they don't see each other. It's sad. It wasn't like that at first, I guess. The surrealists and the clandestine surrealists knew one another. Sometimes they were friends. A few played on both teams: surrealists by day and clandestine surrealists by night. They had their in-jokes, the atmosphere was relaxed. Breton himself dropped a hint about the project, in an interview that's fortunately forgotten today. He said *maybe, maybe, maybe* the time was coming for surrealism to return to the catacombs. *Maybe, maybe, maybe.* Luckily no one took him seriously. What were we talking about?"

"About the telephone selection process, I think."

"It's our way of recruiting people. We can call anywhere in the world. We have a method for fooling the phone companies and not spending anything on the calls. There are CSG associates who are technology whizzes, Diodorus, and this is only the beginning. Then we mark the phone with certain symbols so it can be used for free by immigrants who want to talk to their families in Senegal or Petit Guiana. We never use that phone again. We've got our security measures. Like the urban guerrillas of São Paulo, to give you an idea."

"I think the urban guerrillas of São Paulo are being killed left and right," I said.

"What's killing us, meanwhile, is the heat in summer and the cold in winter. And sometimes boredom, because we're getting old, and boredom is one of the afflictions of old age. I'm going to tell you a story, Diodorus, listen up. At the end of the fifties or the beginning of the sixties, André Breton invited five young surrealists to his house. Four of these surrealists had just arrived in Paris. The fifth was a Parisian and something of an introvert. In other words, he had hardly any friends, or no friends at all. The young men came to Breton's house. There was a Russian, an Italian, a German, and a Spaniard. All of them spoke French, of course. In fact, the German spoke better French than the young Frenchman, who, in addition to being an introvert, stuttered and was dyslexic. So there they are at Breton's house, these five young men, the oldest twenty-two and the youngest eighteen. They're a little bit surprised because Breton's wife and his daughter aren't there, nor are any of the famous surrealists. Famous to the enthusiastic young men, at least, maybe for having published a poem in some magazine that only bibliophiles remember today, or some so-called surrealist collection since fallen into oblivion. You know, the court of mediocrities that kings must suffer."

"But Breton wasn't a king," I protested.

"You're right, he wasn't. A chancellor, then. Or Minister of Foreign Affairs, agreed?"

"Yes," I said.

"Listen up. Here we have these five young men and all of a sudden Breton appears. He greets each of them by name. He acts as if he knows them very well. He asks them questions. He nods. The young men are just as he had imagined. They spend the afternoon together. Then they go out to eat. They wander the streets of Paris. A Paris that is dying, Diodorus, a Paris whose scepter shines on the other side of the ocean, in New York. But they walk the streets of Paris and talk about everything. The young men feel urgency in Breton's words, the radiance of a plan that has yet to be revealed to them. Finally, they go into a café, any old café, where Breton asks whether they're willing to go down into the sewers and live there for ten years. The young men think Breton is speaking figuratively. He repeats the question. The young men reply with other questions. What kind of sewers? The sewers of Paris? The sewers of the mind? The sewers of art? Breton doesn't answer. They drink. They talk about other things. Then they pay and go out. They're lost again in the maze of a bustling old neighborhood. Suddenly, in a side street full of the graffiti of minor political groups, Breton indicates a wooden door and they go into a room. It looks like a toy maker's warehouse. The room has a door that leads to another room, which in turn has a door that leads to another room. And so on. The young men even spot fishing gear along the way. Breton has a bundle of keys that he uses to open all the doors. Finally, they reach the last room. Here the only door is the one they've come through. But then Breton leads them into a corner and opens a trapdoor. They climb down. First Breton, who picks up a flashlight hanging by the top steps, and then the five young men. They reach an octagonal room. Surprised, they hear the rush of water, confirming that they're inside the Paris sewer system. On the walls of the room, a painter or mongoloid child has drawn some chalk figures half-blotted out by the damp. Breton asks again whether they're prepared to live for ten years in the sewers. The young men listen, their eyes on his, and then they look again at the chalk drawings. They all say yes. They leave the room with Breton in the lead once more. When they reach the first room—or the last, depending how you look at it; the one that looks like a toy maker's warehouse—he takes four sets of keys out of a box and presents them to four of the young men, giving his own set to the fifth. Then he shakes each of their hands and says goodbye. The young men are left alone. For a few seconds, they stand there motionless, staring at each other. Then the Russian locks the door and they return to the sewers."

Suddenly the man who was talking on the other end of the line, the man calling from Paris, was silent, as if describing this scene (or remembering it, maybe) had exhausted him. I could hear him breathing. I thought he was having some kind of asthma attack, or heart attack.

"Are you all right?" I asked.

"Perfectly fine . . . Perfectly fine . . ."

Then he coughed or cleared his throat noisily and was silent again. After a few seconds, he began to hum a tune, some French pop song that had yet to reach Guiana, where music arrived from the United States before it arrived from France or Italy or Germany, if music even existed in those countries.

"Where were we?" he asked suddenly.

"With the young men who decided to stay in the sewers."

"Of course. Listen up. Those young men stay in the sewers and form the nucleus of the Clandestine Surrealist Group. Of course, they can come out whenever they want. Did I tell you that each of them has a set of keys that will let them exit at any time?"

"Yes."

"In other words, they aren't prisoners. No one is in charge. They realize this immediately. Not even Breton, who gives away his own set of keys before he leaves. They're free to leave, go back to their garrets, take a train and lose themselves forever in the stations of Europe. In fact, some nights they do go out. They're young. They're more or less able-bodied. They have needs that can't be satisfied in the sewers. Sometimes they attend gatherings with the surrealists and they shake Breton's hand. He's cordial with them, as attentive as ever, but they never talk about the CSG. Breton sees them but doesn't see them. Breton remembers them but doesn't remember them. They meet people, of course. They meet Nora Mitrani, who sees them but doesn't see them. They meet Alain Jouffroy, who sees them but doesn't see them. They talk to Joyce Mansour. Joyce Mansour sees them but doesn't see them. Not that it matters to her. Well, she fucks one of them. You have no idea, Diodorus, how beautiful Joyce Mansour was. They talk to José Pierre, Roberto Matta, Jean Schuster, sometimes they get to be friendly with them, the point is, they have a social life, they go to the movies, they join a gym and learn how to box, they sleep with girls, one of them sleeps with boys, sometimes in summer they take trips to the Adriatic or the Norwegian fjords. Don't get the wrong impression: they don't do all of this together, certainly not, each of them has his own set of keys, they go out on their own, sometimes they might go months without seeing one another, because the sewers are as big as Paris, an inside-out Paris, except that in this private Paris, instead of citizens there are the waste products of citizens, their excreta, their urine, their tears, their sweat, their semen, their vomit, their fetuses, their blood, in other words, the shadow of those citizens, their tenacious shadow, one might add, and the only risk that our five young men run in their investigations—and it's a small risk—is coming across groups of municipal employees, sewer inspectors, drain decloggers who regularly venture down into the labyrinthine city and who are very easy to detect, because the decloggers are afraid of the methane gases that accumulate in blind galleries and they take great precautions. Their shouts, Diodorus, can be heard miles away. The shouts of the decloggers. Their laughter, their jokes, their eagerness to finish the work and get out. Our young men, meanwhile, are in no hurry at all. They know that their work will never be finished. That's why in the summer they run off without a peep. There is one rule that they agree to follow, though they don't always stick to it. Like in hospitals, one person must always be on guard. Four go out, one stays behind. No big deal. The one who stays behind keeps working. And so do those who go out, in some sense. And so the work, the project, begins to take shape, branches, grows, though not in linear fashion. It's like a novel, to give you some sense, a novel that doesn't begin at the beginning. In fact, Diodorus, it's a novel (like all novels, really) that doesn't begin in the novel, in the book-object that contains it, understand? Its first pages are in some other book, or in a back alley where a crime has been committed, or in a bird that watches a group of children playing, unseen."

"Clear as day," I said.

"Which means that our young men discover that they can be away from the sewers as much as they like. The work travels with them. They can be tourists, go to Greece or the Philippines, they can spend weeks paddling the Amazon, what a delight to paddle the Amazon with eyes half-shut, life sighing and creaking around you; to sleep in hammocks, listening to women talking to little girls in Portuguese. In fact, Diodorus, listen up, the five young men soon discover that it isn't necessary to live in the sewers of Paris. It's enough to visit one day a month. And yet the sewer system has become a well-furnished metaphor for them. They have their workshops there, their studies, their libraries. They discuss the possibility of leaving, of course. Each of them proposes a different place. But in the end, they stay. Oh, woe is me, in the end, they stay."

For a while I didn't hear anything. I got the sense that the man on the other end of the line had begun to cry or that he was sighing one sigh after another.

"Where do you think they get the money to lead this life, to live like pashas and bums?" he asked suddenly with renewed vigor.

"I don't know," I admitted.

"The same question was on their minds back then. Because they had money, I can promise you that. Once a month, in one of the rooms on the way to their lair, they would find an envelope containing a not insignificant sum that they divided among the five of them. At first, the logical thing—because logic, Diodorus, is like a madhouse—was to think that Breton was financing them. The work in which they were immersed was absorbing and soon they stopped thinking about it. All they knew for certain was that they had more than enough money to support themselves and to indulge in some Oriental luxuries, though at this point in the story two of them were living practically like clochards. But in 1966, Breton dies and for the first few months they speculate about the possibility that their funding will dry up. The money, however, continues to arrive punctually. So they raise the question again. Who is paying? Who is financing them? Who has an interest in seeing their work continue? Naturally, their thoughts turn to the CIA, the KGB, the French Ministry of Culture. After a quick examination of these possibilities, they rule them out as absurd. The group is clearly opposed to the KGB and the CIA. For several nights after dinner, as they smoke and drink cognac or whiskey, they speculate that the Minister of Culture has gone mad. Try to imagine: these young men spend the day alone, apart, working in the mysterious boulevards and streets of the sewers, and when night falls they turn on their flashlights and walk, maybe whistling as they go, to the first room they glimpsed, the room that Breton showed them. Here they shower, or not; they change clothes, or not; and they sit down at the table. One of them serves as cook. Usually it's the Frenchman, the Italian, or the Spaniard. Sometimes—rarely—it's the Russian. Never the German. Also, it isn't a regular occurrence. It only happens when they have something urgent to discuss, a nightmare to explain, for example, or the last piece of a puzzle to find. Someone is financing them. That someone isn't Breton, since he's dead. Nor is it an American or Soviet spy agency. But someone is in on their secret and possesses a set of keys, since the money isn't found under the door of the toy warehouse but in an inner room, which can only be reached by going through two or three locked doors. For days they ponder the mystery. They lie in wait for the visitor, they set traps for him, they hide inside a wardrobe waiting for him to come. But their capitalist partner, who seems to have a special sense for detecting their presence, doesn't fall into any of the traps. They build a curious system of mirrors by which they intend to get a glimpse of him, and which essentially involves bouncing a reflection from one mirror to another through a keyhole. Finally, after all their attempts fail, they watch a detective movie and realize that the solution is as simple as installing a movie camera in a hidden spot. And they obtain satisfactory results, Diodorus."

"What are the results? Who is bringing them the money?" I asked.

"A woman. An older woman. The picture is a little out of focus. After they develop the film, all they see is a door opening and a woman dressed in black, her face covered with a silk veil, taking two small steps and removing an envelope from a bag. Then the woman retreats, and that's all. The next month, they install two cameras. Same scene, but longer and with one fundamental difference. The woman who enters is dressed in black, her face covered with a veil, but it isn't the woman from the month before. It's a different person. Shorter, maybe; heavier and less quick. Suddenly, our five young men realize that everything, the female backers included, are part of the same project. They keep filming. The woman who turns up in the third month is extremely tall, wearing black pants and a black turtleneck sweater. Instead of a hat, she has on a beret. There is a black satin handkerchief over her face, not a veil. In the fourth month, it's a little old lady who can barely stand upright, though she carries herself with pride and a certain style—call it the smoldering embers of style. Her dress is black, her face is covered with black tulle, her parchment-like wrists display bracelets of incalculable value. In the fifth month, the woman is young, though by the way she walks—the young men watch over and over again, like children spellbound by a western—her experience with love and maybe crime too, is plain. This woman is wearing dark glasses instead of a veil and this permits them to divine the deadly iciness of her gaze. Her gaze, we might add, is her cheekbones and lips. In the sixth month, the woman is wearing dark glasses too and the rest of her face and head are covered with a turban. She is tall and her movements are precise, though there is something shy about her. When she leaves the envelope of money, the young men notice her hands and realize that she is black. In the seventh month, the woman arrives singing. She interrupts her ditty only to bring a handkerchief to her nose and blow. The veil is pushed to one side, and she fixes it with the clumsiness of someone who's had too much to drink. Her black dress is wrinkled and her hat looks as if it's made of paper. She might very well have slept in her clothes. Her eyes, which the veil can't conceal, shine with the determination of someone punching and scratching her way down a long corridor of dreams. And so on, until a year has gone by. Then the first woman appears again, followed by the second, and the third, and so on consecutively. At this point, the young men decide to follow them. The project of pursuit is complicated and involves leaving a trail of bread crumbs or pebbles, except that they can't drop the bread crumbs or pebbles themselves, since the women seem to possess a sixth sense that alerts them to their proximity, so it's the women who must drop them. After a while this flurry of activity bears fruit. The three women whom they've followed turn out to be surrealist widows. Two of them are the widows of painters whose work is rising in value on the international market. The third is the widow of a poet possessing a large family fortune. When they follow the fourth, it turns out that she too is the widow of a painter. They find the others by means of a much simpler system: they track down the surrealists who left lots of money when they died and then they go in search of the widows. The next step is to turn up at the house of one of these widows and interrogate her about why the women are covering their expenses, but they decide not to take this step, because somehow they feel the time is not yet right. Once this problem has been solved, they immerse themselves in their work again. In their masterwork. Do you know what that masterwork is, Diodorus?"

"I have a vague idea, sir. Preparing the revolution? Laying the foundation for the literature of the future?" These must be the right questions to ask, I thought. I didn't want to look like an idiot. I didn't want this man who had called me from Paris to decide all of a sudden that I wasn't a viable contender and hang up on me.

"Cold, cold, but also hot, hot." The voice seemed to recede, as if all of a sudden doors were beginning to close between my interlocutor and me, one after the other, blown shut by a hurricane wind that not only made him shrink but also literally made my hearing dwindle, so that I put a hand up to my ear pressed to the telephone and felt it: it was still the same size, only much hotter than usual.

"I'll tell you about our masterwork and what we expect you to do in the Clandestine Surrealist Group when you come to join us."

"When will that be?" I gasped.

My interlocutor's voice rasped. I heard him spit. I imagined him in an underground gallery, talking on a pirated phone line, his gaze fixed on the river flowing through the gallery toward an enormous treatment system resembling a mill with silver blades.

"In three months. We expect you on July 28, at precisely eight p.m., on the rue de la Réunion, at Père Lachaise Cemetery. Do you have paper and pencil?"

"I have a pen," I said.

"Well, write this down. July 28. Eight p.m. Rue de la Réunion, Père Lachaise Cemetery. If anything goes wrong, head to the rue du Louvre. Walk from rue Saint-Honoré to rue d'Aboukir. A hunchbacked man will approach you and ask how to get to La Promenade de Vénus. Do you know what La Promenade de Vénus is?"

"No."

"It's a café. All right. Listen up. The man with the hunchback will come up to you and ask you where La Promenade de Vénus is. You don't say anything, you raise a finger to your head and touch it, as if to say that the location of the café is a mental thing. Do you understand? Have you written it all down?"

"Yes."

"Very well, Diodorus Pilon, that's all for now."

"But how will I get to Paris?" I asked.

"By plane or by ship, of course."

"I don't have any money," I almost shouted.

For a few seconds, I couldn't hear anything. I worried that the sharpness of my cry might have seemed rude.

"Are you still there, sir?" I asked.

"I'm thinking, Diodorus, and I don't know what to tell you. We can't send you the ticket from here. We can't send you money, either. It would be a violation of our security measures. You'll have to handle getting the ticket. When you're in Paris, we can cover your costs, but you'll have to pay for the trip yourself."

"Don't worry, sir, I'll be at Père Lachaise Cemetery on July 28," I said, somewhat recovered and without a clue where I would get money for the ticket.

"Not at the cemetery, Diodorus, on rue de la Réunion, on rue de la Réunion, for Christ's sake, get it into your head."

"On rue de la Réunion, no problem."

"All right, you have a good life, goodbye."

And he hung up.

I stood there without moving, not knowing whether to laugh or pinch myself, with the phone in my hand as day began to dawn around me. The light that came in through the glass walls of the phone booth had a tentative pallor, conjuring up the green of the hills and the pearly color of the sea first thing in the morning. It was as if I were inside a transparent submarine, a little submarine that had been down to the bottom of an ocean trench. Now, back on the surface again, I was afraid to open the door and emerge.

A man came out of one of the nearby houses. He was wearing a light-colored suit and carrying his jacket in one hand, in a jaunty yet fastidious way, with a leather briefcase in his other hand. He was wearing a short-sleeved white shirt. His arms were long and strong, like a professional swimmer's. Maybe he was a college professor or a government official. He looked at me as if trying to place me and then he got in his car and started it. As he passed the phone booth, he turned to stare at me and I returned his gaze. When the car was gone I came out of the booth and set off for the Coves. By now my poor mother would be gone, but I felt like taking a walk before I went home.

As I headed downhill through the Old Hospital neighborhood, I saw a man I knew by sight—a big black man with a beaked nose who sometimes played guitar in the port bars or De Gaulle Park—standing in a phone booth, listening without saying a word, and sweating rivers.

All the beach stands were shut. The sand, which later in the day would be yellow, now looked as if it was covered by a white sheet or a shroud of ash, depending on the spot. I ran into a drunk, someone to whom my mother would give plates of fried fish. He had just woken up.

"Hey kid, what are you doing out so early in the morning?" he asked.

"I haven't been to bed yet, Achille," I said.

I sat down next to him on the seawall and listened to his stories for a while. He told me that the night before, as I was talking on the phone to Paris, a cat had gone crazy and had to be shot and killed. He said that the eclipse thing wasn't such a big deal and that people were always getting excited about nothing. In his opinion, true and incredible things happened in the sky every day, but all a man needed was a good woman by his side. You could do without everything else, except that. As we talked, I saw three figures appear at the other end of the street, weaving along. I thought they must be drunks, maybe friends of Achille, in search of a bed or a hospital. As they got closer, I realized that it was the well-dressed guy who had danced at the House of the Sun during the eclipse, with the two women. He didn't look as well-dressed as he had before. His suit was ripped in places and he had lost his tie. The older woman's clothes were in more or less the same state. Only the girl looked as if she'd had a quiet night. When they reached us, the girl asked if we knew the address of a cheap boarding-house where they could stay. Achille eyed them curiously and then asked the girl what had happened to the other two.

"They've gone blind," she said.

"How did that happen?" asked Achille.

"They spent too long staring at the black sun," she said.

"The black sun?"

"The eclipse," I said.

"Oh, well, that makes sense, then," said Achille, and he gave the girl an address on avenue Kennedy, where boardinghouses and cheap hostels followed one after the other. "Make sure you tell the owner that Achille sent you," he said in farewell.

FATHERLAND

Fatherland

My father was a boxing champion: the bravest, the fiercest, the smartest, the best . . .

When he gave up boxing, Police Commissioner Carner of Concepción offered him a job in Investigations. My father laughed and said no, where the hell did he get an idea like that. The chief replied that he could smell an officer of the law from a distance. His nose never failed him. My father said he didn't give a shit for the law and also, no offense, he didn't see himself as a freeloader. I like to work, he said, don't take it the wrong way. The chief realized that my father might be drunk but he was serious. No offense taken, he said, it's just strange, because I can smell a cop ten miles off. The good kind, of course. Don't give me that shit, Carner, what you want is a heavyweight to beat up purse snatchers, said my father. Never, said the commissioner, I'm a modern lawman. Modern or not, Carner read the Rosicrucians and he was a follower (in a casual way) of John William Burr, the now-forgotten promoter of metempsychosis.

At home, we still have pamphlets by Burr, published by El Círculo in Valparaiso and the Gustavo Peña Association in Lima, which my father, predictably, never read.

As far as I can remember, my father only read the sports news. He had an album of clippings and pictures that he meticulously maintained, tracking his pugilistic journey from the ranks of amateur boxing to the bronze belt in the South American heavyweight championships. (He also liked football and horse races and *tejo*—the Columbian version of lawn bowls, played with explosives—and cocaine and swimming and cowboy movies . . .)

My father never joined the police force, of course. When he retired, he opened a soda fountain and married my mother, who was three months pregnant. Soon after, I was born, the poet of the family.

The Family Idiot

It all began years ago, on September 11, 1973, at seven a.m., in the library of the country house of Antonio Narváez, a well-known gynecologist and a patron of the fine arts in his spare time. Before my sleep-reddened eyes, twenty people lay sprawled on the sofas and rugs! All had drunk and argued without cease that night! All had laughed and made plans and danced without cease that interminable night! Except for me. Then, at seven or eight a.m., at the request of our host and his wife, I climbed onto a chair and began to recite a poem to lift everyone's spirits and pass the time while the coffee was brewing, the exceptionally fine coffee that Antonio Narváez procured on the black market and served with restorative shots of pisco or whiskey before opening the curtains and letting in the first rays of sun as dawn broke over the Andes.

Well, I got up on the chair and the master and mistress of the house called for a moment of silence! This was my specialty. The reason I was invited to parties. Before an audience of familiar faces from the University of Concepción, faces glimpsed at film screenings or plays or encountered at previous country affairs, at the literary ambushes that Dr. Narváez liked to organize, I recited one of Nicanor Parra's greatest poems from memory. My voice shook. As I gesticulated, my hands shook. But I still think it was a good poem, though it was received with pleasure by some and manifest disapproval by others. I remember that when I climbed up on the chair I realized that I, too, had drunk like a Cossack the night before. The chair was made of araucaria wood and, from up above, the rug's arabesques seemed infinitely distant.

I must have been on the fifteenth stanza when two guys and a girl came in from the kitchen and broke the news. The radio was reporting that a military coup was underway in Santiago. Blitzkrieg or Anschluss, call it what you want, the Chilean Army was on the move.

The minute the announcement was made, the stampede was on, first into the kitchen and then toward the front door, as if everyone had suddenly gone mad.

I remember that in the middle of the scramble someone yelled at me to shut up, by which I gather that I was still reciting. I remember insults, threats, exclamations of disbelief, expressions mutating from the most sublime heroism to terror and back again, everything topsy-turvy and unfinished, while I stuttered over a line and scanned every corner, the last to realize what was looming over the republic. In the avalanche of people fleeing, my chair tottered and I fell flat on my face.

The impact was sharp and painless. Half-stunned, I wondered why it was taking me so long to pass out. Then everything went black.

When I came to, the house was empty except for a girl whose lap my head was resting on. I didn't recognize her right away. But it wasn't the first time I'd seen her. We'd spoken the night before, and we'd met a few times before that at some workshop, Fernández's or Cherniakovski's, I wasn't sure which.

A wet cloth was draped over my forehead and it was giving me the shivers. Someone had opened the curtains. An upstairs shutter was swinging in the wind, making a sound like a metronome. In the library, there was something supernatural about the way the silence and light enveloped us: the air seemed different, bright, new, an amalgam of superimposed walls behind which lay adventure or death. I looked at the clock. Only ten minutes had gone by. Then she said, Get up, we have to go as soon as we can. Like a ghost, I got up. Light as a ghost, I mean. Light as a feather. I was twenty years old! I got up and followed her. In the street was a Volkswagen with green bumpers and leopard-skin upholstery. We got in the car and set off. I was twenty and I was falling in love for the first time! I knew it instantly . . . And I couldn't help it, tears came to my eyes . . .

The Right Side

Her name was Patricia Arancibia and she was twenty-one. She lived outside of Nacimiento, town of potters, in a two-story house of stone and wood, at the top of a bald hill with sweeping views of the whole valley. Along the way, I opened my mouth twice: first to ask where we were going, and second to tell her that her eyes were blue like the rivers of the province of Bío-Bío. The province has seven rivers, she said, glancing at me as we drove along dirt roads, speeding away from Los Ángeles. The Mulchén, the Vergara, the Laja, the Renaico, the Bureo, the Duqueco, and the Bío-Bío, father of them all. And each is different in color and flow. Sometimes, though hardly ever, all seven are blue, with big green tongues in the pools, though most of the time they run the color of stone, dark stone with emerald and violet streaks. Especially when the winter is long, she said sadly.

At first sight, her house looked like the house from *Psycho*. Only the stairs and the views were different. From Patricia

Arancibia's house, the views were sweeping, rich, desolate. From Norman's house, of course, all you could see was the old highway and the swamp.

She parked the car under a shelter of weathered planks. The front door wasn't locked. I followed her into the living room, which was enormous and full of art and books. My father is a painter, said Patricia. These are his paintings. As she made me tea, I looked at them. The central figure in nearly all of them was a woman with features vaguely resembling my rescuer's. She's my mother, Patricia explained, handing me a cup of tea. At a word from her, I sat in a chair while she examined my head. You're all right, she said, but it's strange that you were unconscious for so long. Where did everyone else go? I asked. Home, to their party headquarters, to their jobs, I don't know . . . Why did you call the Bío-Bío the father of all rivers, not the mother? Patricia laughed. You should see a doctor, she said. For your head. I feel fine, I said. Once there was a pretty good artist who fell or was hit by a car; anyway, something like what happened to you. They took him to the hospital. After a while, he recuperated, or seemed to. He looked healthy and the nurses let him have paper and pencil. The first thing he wanted to draw was a portrait of an especially nice nurse. The nurse posed for him, flattered. When he was finished, everyone realized that he had only drawn her right half. As a test, they asked him to draw a table. He drew the right half of the table. When the doctors pointed this out to him, he insisted that the drawing was finished and complete. They tried a few more times and the same thing happened. The artist only drew what he saw, and he had lost sight of the left side of things . . .

I see everything whole, I said softly. I see your left side and your right side. The Bío-Bío is the father of all rivers, said Patricia Arancibia, and the Antuco is the mother of all volcanoes. It should be the other way around, I said. Father volcanoes and mother rivers. Patricia Arancibia laughed. I live with a woman who works for my family, she said. Do you know what her name is? It's Crescencia Copahue. She's seventy years old. She was my father's nanny, though actually she's like part of the family. Do you know what Copahue is? No idea, I said. It's a volcano. Copahue is one of the seven volcanoes of Bío-Bío. Haven't you ever seen my father's paintings? No, I said. I've never even heard of him. There were some hot springs on Copahue that we visited when I was little. My father painted volcanoes, years ago. All the canvases have been sold now or burned.

I live alone, she said. My mother and father live in Santiago. They love each other desperately, she said with a smile. I live with Crescencia. She's here now, somewhere in the house, listening to the radio. She must be in bed listening to the military speeches. But she'll get up soon and make us something to eat. Do you know the names of the seven volcanoes of Bío-Bío? Copahue, Tolhuaca, Collapén, Pemehue, Sierra Velluda, Maya-Maya, and Antuco, the most beautiful of all. Why are you closing your eyes? I was imagining the volcanoes, I said. I saw them as walls closing us in. Because of the coup? Don't see them that way, said the sweet voice.

They felt like bars to my father too, bars to his talent, which is maybe why he went to live in Santiago. The artist who could only see the right side of things, is he still alive? No, he died a long time ago, in New York, in the 1930s, before World War II. His name was Richard Luciano and his drawings still turn up in neuropathology papers sometimes. How sad to end up in a medical journal! I said with my eyes full of tears. Not really, said the sweet voice. Better there than in a museum. Life takes many turns, Mr. Belano, the adventure never ends . . .

Which Way Was Patricia Arancibia Driving That Morning? Toward Heaven or Hell?

The spotless Volkswagen glided along the roads of Bío-Bío as if along a conveyor belt. It braked and accelerated at nudges from the sun, the warm rays on the leopard skin. And Patricia Arancibia, with no sunglasses to shade her eyes, surveyed the roads and chose the best. Down tree-lined streets or oxen tracks, along the edge of fields, past Coigüe or Santa Fe, at the hour of the lazy man's call to morning prayer, her slender legs moving confidently in the belly of the leopard, setting the desired speed. She was wearing black leather boots with silver buckles, magenta cotton socks sprinkled with tiny stars, a high-waisted black knee-length skirt—tight as if for horse-riding—a brown silk blouse with round pearly buttons, and, carelessly tossed in the back seat, a 1950s starlet's kid-leather jacket. Every so often she stopped the car in a cloud of dust and consulted a map that she pulled from the glove compartment. The scene was like an advertisement for a savage perfume: her long fingers tracing the roads printed in red, her lips pressed firmly together. Then the car slowly emerged from the cloud of dust as if from an egg. An egg of stone, of light and air, ephemeral as a fly. Volcano egg. And the spotless Volkswagen gradually picked up speed again. Left behind was the shell, crumbling among the tree branches. The map was returned to the glove compartment. Her hands clutched the wheel and the car set off again.

"Where are we going?" I asked in a frightened voice.

(When I was a boy, my siblings and I played a game of turning happy moments into statues . . . If only someone, an angel watching from up above, had turned the Volkswagen and the bumps in the road into a statue . . . The leopard-skin throne into a statue . . . Our speed and our flight into a statue . . .)

She accelerated unhesitatingly. Don't worry, Mr. Belano, she said mockingly, we won't get lost . . . We won't lose anything . . . Her lips, as Virgil's Argentine or Bolivian translator would have it, were full of ambrosia.

From Eliseo Arancibia
to Rigoberto Belano

I've received four letters from you and I'd say that's enough. Don't grub around in my family's suffering. Don't sully my daughter's memory with conjectures and speculations that lead nowhere. Please, desist. The facts are clear and I don't see why I should believe you and your suspicions over the police report. It was God's will that my daughter be taken from us in the flower of her youth, and that, unfortunately, is that.

As for sending you Patricia's papers, my answer is no. I don't know what papers you're referring to. And if I knew, I'm afraid you wouldn't be the likely recipient. When time has done its healing work, I'll be able to calmly and patiently collect my daughter's scattered writings and publish them in worthy fashion. I have plenty of editor friends. I beg you, therefore, not to appoint yourself literary executor when no one has asked you to do so.

Finally: don't exploit my daughter's disappearance. Not politically, and not literarily. On this point, I find myself obliged to insist. You have no right. Patricia despised the commonness that I sense in your intentions. I don't need to tell you that if it comes down to it, I won't hesitate to take legal steps.

If my words are harsh, I'm sorry. Please understand, I'm a heartbroken father. You, on the other hand, are a young man and you ought to think of your future.

I enclose our magazine *Chilean Painters Here and Abroad*, with a profile of Onésimo Echaurren that you may enjoy.

Funeral Oration Read by the Interim Secretary of the Chilean Society of Fine Arts, the Honorable Mr. Onésimo Echaurren Gordon. Published in the Quarterly Journal *Chilean Painters Here and Abroad*, 1974, and Excerpted in the Obituaries Section of *El Mercurio*, 1973. Unabridged.

We are gathered here, friends and colleagues, in tribute to a fragile rose, to the still-fresh petals of the loveliest of flowers, the lushest and most enigmatic of flowers, torn too soon from the breast of Nature: mother of us all, the blind and the sighted, the creators and the creatures of the night, the artist who sees and transcends, and that hideous Afro-Haitian spawn, the zombie.

Just when it seemed that the terrible drought was lifting, when the clamor of vulturine flocks seeking to clip the wings of our beloved condor was vanishing like a bad dream from the Nation's frozen breast, when Andean deer were frolicking once again in reclaimed valleys, and when the tolling of bells announced to young and old that the Republic was forging ahead with new vigor and verve, the news reached our homes like the night's final blow, tragic news plunging us without warning into a private tempest.

I can say that I was there at her birth; friendship, that sacred, mysterious bond, afforded me the happy privilege of watching her grow up. How can I help but call to mind her little face as it looked in the light of my four copper lamps (they were more like torches), begging me to tell her yet another story, one more in a long list. Unforgettable evenings, wreathed in the magnificent light of the province of Temuco, at La Refalosa, my country estate, the name of which does not harbor a grammatical error, as some of my enemies have insinuated, but rather the pure folk wisdom of my elders, which I'm honored to preserve.

As if time, forgetful friend, hadn't wagged its comet tail, I seem to see onstage before me the spacious veranda at La Refalosa, with easels at the ready, palettes prepared, paints set out; beyond is the garden, and at the edge of the garden, the children, playing cowboys (children who today are students of Law or Economics!); the countryfolk, humbly attired but generally clean and of cheerful mien, are on their way to the tilled fields; and here she comes, our precocious eight-year-old Amazon, Venus of Botticelli, Max Ernst's magical woman-child, Alberto Ortega Basauri's sulky divine thing, riding my mare Dusty through the roses.

Blessed vision! Her winged presence produced something akin to astonishment, of the sort usually elicited only by poems, whether on canvas or on the page. Abstracted traveler of imaginary lands, from the very start she dazzled her dear parents and the select circle to which they belonged with her intellect and beauty. I can say without hesitation that it was from Eliseo Arancibia that she inherited her open, unwavering intelligence, and from Elena Múgica Echevarría the beauty and grace that were hers until the final dusk.

As evidence of her cleverness, let me say that by the age of ten she could already hold forth on the vagaries of criollo and French surrealism. She valued the work of our dear Juan Miguel Marot, of blessed memory, and she dispelled any confusion about the overvalued paintbrush of Roberto Antonio Matta. Spellbound, the grown-ups—our fun-loving *Here and Abroad* gang, who back then were just skimming the edge of their forties (oh, happy age!)—heard her say in her deep, confident little voice, her body leaning like a Harlequin on her beloved father's knee, that Leonora Carrington's main defect was her dreadful thinness.

As I've said, she was blessed with her father's talent and the beauty of the woman who bore her, but there was something else, something visible only to the artist's discerning eye, if I may say so: a quality of character (and character, as everyone knows, is the seat of talent, its palace and its lair), a quality of character, as I was saying, that was singular, unique, incommutable. Chiseled in fire. It was a Chilean quality, but English too, something to astound the shrewdest psychologist.

She had it all (or all that anyone can have by the age of twenty-one), but she wasn't spoiled. A good daughter, a good student, a good friend, steadfast in everything that she undertook, free as a bird; sometimes my tired eyes seemed to see a human being with a lifetime of experiences and vicissitudes, not a person—an exquisite person—born in 1952. Such was her kindness and her sweetness, her understanding and her grace.

I saw her for the last time eight or nine months before her death, at her father's opening at the Círculo Francés of Santiago. It goes without saying that she was a grown woman by then. As always, she exuded life and talent from every pore. We exchanged a few words. I learned that she was studying literature at the University of Concepción, that she wrote poems (I begged her to recite one on the spot, but she modestly declined, judging it unseemly), that she was planning to travel to Europe at the end of the year, that she lived alone or rather with her old Mapuche nurse at her enchanted and enchanting house in Nacimiento, that it had been a while since she gave up drawing. I thought this was a shame, and she graced me with one of her frank, crystalline laughs, ripe with health.

After the opening, we threw a party for Eliseo at the home of the Ortega Basauris. Some among us will still remember the event with fondness and nostalgia. Present were new and old members of the group of *Here and Abroad* painters, joined in fruitful camaraderie. The times were tumultuous, but we were undaunted. Patricia turned up too, though just for a moment, with her parents and a friend with whom she planned to leave for Viña del Mar. Surrounded as I was by reporters and strangers asking my opinion on a wide range of topics, it was impossible for us to approach each other. After a while, she and her friend were gone and Eliseo himself conveyed her goodbyes.

Did I suspect, perhaps, that it would be the last time?

Who knows!

All I know is that I cried like a child when, months later, Eliseo called to give me the news. And in my cathartic weeping, I was accompanied by my wife and my son, Juan Carlos.

She's gone. She has flown far from our woes and tribulations. She is no longer with us. God has deprived us of her laughter and her gaze. We've all lost. The whole of Chile has lost. Her death might seem the best argument for discouragement.

And yet it's necessary to carry on. Carry on, we must! Now more than ever.

I'll conclude by saying that Patricia loved the night. She loved it for the gift and consolation of the stars, she confessed to me and her father one distant (pure and distant) day, on the sprawling veranda of La Refalosa, sipping a cold tea after a tiring excursion. In the vast night, the same night in which all of us will be lost, the stars twinkle. That's our Southern Cross. Beyond it, the firmament extends its mantle of orbs and lights. That's where Patricia lives. She's waiting for us there.

The Biggest.
The Border-Maker.
The Prettiest River at the
Ass End of the Earth.

These aren't the roads of the counterrevolution, said Patricia Arancibia, as I quaked. These are the roads of Los Ángeles, Nacimiento, the province of Bío-Bío. We're on our way to my house.

The Messerschmitt

In December, a few lucky people saw the old plane flying over Concepción. It was the time of day when the sun sinks into the Pacific, rolling toward the islands, the happy places, toward Japan and the Philippines. The plane appeared from the north, as if approaching from Tomé. It came in over Talcahuano and spent a long time circling over Concepción. I was in the police station gymnasium, now a holding pen for political prisoners, recovering from my last beating, and I don't know where I got the strength to come to the window; where I got the idea that it was important to see that plane.

It was Gaspar Yáñez who said that a Messerschmitt was flying over the city. A what? A Messerschmitt, comrades, a Third Reich fighter plane, let me get a good look at it, a 109, the crown jewel of the Luftwaffe, two 15-mm machine guns and a 30-mm cannon. What's it doing? the prisoners asked. For a few seconds, Gaspar Yáñez studied the red rectangle in silence . . . Aerobatics! Spins! Loops! Rolls! The pilot must be ecstatic!

I remember that the light inside the gymnasium was a dusky yellow and every face was turned toward Gaspar Yáñez, who was peering out the window like a pirate. Christ almighty, what a pilot, what a plane, what a sight! Sitting on the floor, the men and women listened in silence: Gaspar's thin, bony face, his broad nose and full lips, seemed to smolder in the red of the sunset. They were the fighter planes in the Battle of England, he said as if in prayer. Wait until a Hawker Hunter turns up and see what happens to your fighter, spat someone from a dark corner. Never was so much owed by so many to so few, added the dean of the Law School, who was dozing on a filthy mattress between two miners from Lota.

But this one seems to be retrofitted, said Gaspar. Look, there's smoke coming from it! The beauty of it, gentlemen! The elegance, the grace! Don't bad-mouth German technology to me! Does the smoke mean it's going down, Gasparcito? asked a woman of about fifty, also from Lota. Going down? No! It's writing something in the sky. Holy mother, what can it be, what can it be, cried Gaspar in agony. It must be an advertisement, said one of the prisoners. Then I leaped over the blankets, the mattresses, and the bodies and I looked out the window.

Through the bars, I saw the plane, the silent propellers, the square-tipped wings, just like in *Spitfire* magazine, the steel-blue enemy fighter plane, strangely lovely. And then I saw the words: the bold script swiftly whittled away by the wind, the dark text written in the sky as if by someone with the secret wish to be read only in a mirror. And the lines of poetry, words that I had heard before, stolen—like so much else—from Patricia Arancibia's house.

It's advertising a volcanic drink! cried Gaspar Yáñez, who was raving by now. It's announcing the birth of Fascist literature, comrades!

Shut up, you crazy bastard, called a chorus of protesters, irritable miners.

Across the city, two helicopters appeared, painted camouflage green. They were flying low, just over the rooftops, and they were approaching the edge of the area where the plane was performing its maneuvers. I felt the air vibrate. Dogfight! shouted Gaspar. No one paid any attention to him. Behind us the silence was startling. I turned around: the prisoners were talking, eating, sleeping, playing checkers with scraps of paper, thinking. The Chilean Air Force versus the Luftwaffe! Helicopters of Quiriquina Island! Onward, boys! shouted Gaspar. He began to foam at the mouth, his body shaking with spasms that grew more and more violent. It took four men to get him away from the window. I didn't move. The helicopters were just below the Messerschmitt. This kid needs a doctor, said someone, or at least a painkiller. The voice was cool as could be. A woman from the Lota group pulled a little box of pills from her bra and handed one to the person tending to Gaspar. Now Gaspar's moans sounded like the thunder before a storm.

But not a Chilean storm: an African storm. With deep sadness, I watched the flurry of blankets, the hands grasping Gaspar's jaw, the contradictory opinions flying back and forth, the shadows of the gymnasium: we truly seemed more like lunatics than prisoners.

When I looked out the window again, the helicopters were heading back to their bases. In Concepción's inflamed sky, the plane made a last pirouette and then it rose proudly and was lost in the clouds . . . Gaspar began to pull out clumps of hair. The gray words were left behind in the red sky, dissolving in the air.

The Crown Jewel of
the Luftwaffe

It was the best plane in the world, in the darkness of the world, said Gaspar Yáñez, on all fours like a mythological beast at death's door; his voice, the succession of syllables in my ear, woke me with a start. Everyone is asleep, said Gaspar Yáñez. The vowels fell petrified from his lips by the dark and by fear. A perpendicular movement made him rock from knees to wrists. It's strange, don't you think? Muted voices and laughter reached us; the sound of water flowing from a hose. What's strange? I whispered even more softly than the madman, so softly that I was afraid he wouldn't hear me, but he heard. The plane, he said. The fighter circling over our heads. I repeated what others had explained already, that the FACh kept a German plane as a museum piece, that it had been in Chile since approximately 1939, but as I was talking I realized that I didn't believe the explanation either. Gaspar smiled (on the second day of his detention, they had broken most of his teeth) as if he could guess what I was thinking. I heard the laughter and the gush of water again, I imagined the snaking of the hose in the prison yard. They're having fun, said Gaspar, as if he wanted to lay the subject to rest and move on to what was really important. Who? The cops. They never sleep, it must be their consciences, or a sixth sense warning them of Solitude. Those thugs have no conscience, I said. Gaspar sighed. His lungs made a very strange sound. I think the world is full of holes, he said, and that's how the fighter planes get in. Have you heard me talk about Solitude? (Strange question.) Another hole, that's all. I don't believe in that kind of thing, I whispered. You don't have to believe, said Gaspar, I've seen the planes flying at dawn and it's not a matter of believing or not. When you see the silhouettes in the cabins, the face of Hans Marseille like a crumb of white bread, you realize that it's the only consolation. Consolation for what? I stammered. My vocal cords were turning to stone too. It's hard to admit, but consolation for everything, said Gaspar. Nothing but the crown jewel of the Luftwaffe up in the sky. The 109, and then all the prototypes, planes even better than the 109, I must confess, though it's the number that makes all the difference. What? What? I whispered. The number of crewmen. Each of the others flies two, my friend, and that's no good. The 109 has room for just one and you really do need balls for that. Take off from France, climb above the clouds, and reach England in time to fight for five minutes in a wind made of dreams. What are you talking about, man? I whispered. Weren't you a radio host? Weren't you on that show *Bring in the Kids*? Are you so crazy that you've turned into a Nazi? Gaspar gave me a horrible smile, shaking his head. Then he raised one hand and patted me on the shoulder. Without getting up, he vanished on all fours into the darkness toward his mat. For a long time I lay awake. The next day, they brought me out into the courtyard, gave me a beating, and tossed me into the street.

Family Plot

Effects of the coup on the family unit. My mother lost her job as a math teacher at Liceo number 3 in Concepción. My father and my mother were on speaking terms again. My brother David was arrested and beaten: for fifteen days my parents searched for him at police stations and hospitals. He came home a month later and for the next thirty days he refused to say a word. My mother wept and cried out, asking what they'd done to her son. My father watched him, touched him, stared into his face, and declared that whatever it was, it wouldn't kill him. My sister Elisenda was angry all of the time. Meals were scanty, but now at least the whole family sat down to eat together. My father came over from across the street and we all ate together at my mother's house. Or my mother and the three of us crossed the street and we all ate together at my father's house. My sister Elisenda stopped watching so much TV. My brother David started to train every morning in the yard. He was taking a martial arts correspondence course: karate, kung fu, judo. When my father was at my mother's house, he spied on my brother through the kitchen window and smiled. In front of my mother, my sister, and me, my brother David said that he could drop my father with a single karate kick. Frankly, everyone in the family was on edge. More and more, my mother wondered why we still lived in this country. My father, who used to criticize the Allende government for its sports policies, stopped talking about sports for a while. My brother David became a Trotskyite. My sister Elisenda burned her childhood books and then cried bitterly. My father tried to make love to my mother five or six times, and the results, to judge by their faces, were not satisfactory. My mother got out her songbook and played the guitar. My father closed the soda fountain and sold it soon after to a retired navy sergeant. When my brother David was arrested for the second time and my sister saw her chances of enrolling in the university vanishing, my mother said that enough was enough. She sold the house and the furniture and bought tickets to Lima. She would have liked to get tickets to Madrid, but she didn't have enough money. She cried when I refused to go with them. My brother David called me a faggot and a eunuch. I replied that I might be a faggot, you never know, but I definitely wasn't a eunuch. Maliciously I added that, according to my father, it was people who practiced martial arts imported from the East who were eunuchs. My brother David tried to hit me. Don't hit him in the head, my mother cried. The days before the departure were like the rosary of the dawn. My brother David made up with me. David, Elisenda, and I hugged. I promised my mother that I would save some money and come join them. I promised that I'd stay out of trouble. My father and I accompanied my mother and siblings to Santiago. As the plane took off, my father muttered to himself and bit his knuckles. I understood how he felt. I imagined my mother and my brother and sister in their seats, with their seat belts on, sad but full of energy, defying the future and what it held in store for them, no matter what. My father, however, seemed to be on the verge of death, his face shrunken, as if he had inner wrinkles now in addition to his outer ones. Never had he looked more like a famous boxer than he did then. We took the train back to Concepción. For the trip, my father bought a roast chicken and a bottle of wine. We ate and drank in fits and starts, I don't know why. My father didn't sleep a wink. Sometimes I was woken by the sound of him sucking on a wing. A very strange noise. He picked up the wing in his hand and sucked on it slowly, his gaze lost in the darkness of the car. I'll never see them again, my father said. Two weeks later, the first postcards arrived. My mother's postcard was fairly optimistic. My brother's was more like a riddle or a puzzle. I could never figure out the clues, if there were any. My sister's was the most idiotic, but at the same time I liked it best, maybe because it was so innocent. Basically, it described the trip from Santiago to Lima. The part she liked best was the movie she saw on the plane: Hitchcock's *Family Plot*.

The Dream

It was years after Patricia Arancibia's death that I began to dream about the dark city . . . A kid, seventeen, walked the empty streets, flanked by tall buildings . . . His strides were long, almost feline . . . I can't say why, but I'm sure he was seventeen . . . I'm also sure of his bravery . . . He was wearing a white shirt and loose black pants that flapped in the wind like a flag . . . He was wearing sneakers that had once been white but in the dream were an indeterminate color . . . He had long hair and though his face remained in shadow I glimpsed dark wolf or coyote eyes . . . The streets were vast, some paved, some cobbled, but vast and empty . . . The kid loped along, happy to be alive, happy that the warm wind was rippling his clothes . . . Then four or five people appeared . . . They all knew one another and they walked together for a while . . . Next the kid and his companions stopped at an overlook . . . Beneath them was a ravine, and, in the distance, the silhouettes of other buildings . . . Among the buildings rose the movie theater, imposing as four cathedrals and four soccer fields . . . The Diorama . . . The kid and his companions admired the dark landscape and produced bottles of beer and drugs from somewhere . . . Little by little their gestures became more disturbing . . . They gesticulated, argued . . . One of the guys, fat and wearing tight pants, grabbed the kid by the neck and hurled him into the middle of the street . . . The others laughed . . . Then a knife appeared in the kid's hand and he stepped toward the fat guy . . . No one saw anything, but the laughter froze . . . The fat guy took the blow in the stomach . . . He could feel the tension in the kid's arm . . . The kid's determination, edged with disgust . . . Disgust conquered by the driving force of his arm . . . Then the storm began . . .

A Drink on the Road

Cherniakovski? Juan Cherniakovski? Iván Cherniakovski? Cherniakovski, the poet. I remember him, said the algebra teacher, nobody who saw him even once could forget Cherniakovski. He was as handsome as they come. Back then, in '71 or '72, the ladies were always chasing him, you know? I'm no faggot, one look at me and it's obvious I don't give a shit about fashion, but I had eyes or at least I could see things more clearly back then, vision's going, you know? Though ideologically everything is as dark as ever, if that makes sense, I guess confusion is just our natural state, the natural state of history, I don't know, Slim, sometimes I think it would make the most sense for all of us to kill ourselves, but luckily I've got my old lady and the goats and I'm still down in the trenches. What was I saying? Cherniakovski, Juanito Cherniakovski, a great poet, though I'm no judge, it's been years since I read a poem and to think there was a time when I wrote them. I haven't even read Zurita, which says it all. Not Zurita, not Millán, not Maquieira, though none of them are dead yet. What can I tell you about the ones who went into exile? It's like they never existed. But where was I? Juanito Cherniakovski. Nice guy. Son of the Dead Sea, that was what the Fascists in Econ called him, it's hard to explain how scared people were of him, how much they respected him. Even the nickname, which was supposed to be insulting, is a giveaway. See, they didn't call him a Jew bastard, there's the difference. Honestly, I don't know what it was about Cherniakovski, but people respected him. Don't think for a minute that he was some leftist thug, the kind who were all over the place, unfortunately, or that he ever raised his voice, threatened anybody. I think Cherniakovski won people over with his looks. Go on, laugh. Have you seen any paintings by Dürer, Slim? And do you remember the one called *Oswolt Krel*? You never saw it in your life? It's oil on wood, with two side panels that close over the portrait of Oswolt Krel, and on each of the side panels, along with the family coats of arms, there's a scary-looking wild man with blond hair. But the important thing is the portrait of Oswolt. The spitting image of Cherniakovski! Pure energy! Pure tragic energy, if you know what I mean, Slim. That was Cherniakovski, he had the most tragic, soulful eyes I've ever seen, though I could be exaggerating. I've seen lots of eyes since then, or at least it seems like a lot to me. I've even seen eyes in my soup, Slim! You too? Let's drink to that! Oswolt Krel, God damn it. Juanito Cherniakovski in the flesh . . . Respected, admired, beloved, but a touch of the odd bird, like Oswolt, frankly. A touch of something strange in the eyes. A touch? No, man, I take that back, a shitload. You should see the painting, Slim! Oswolt Krel gets a glimpse of something terrible, yes? And it's obvious that he has, but he restrains himself, he pulls himself together, it's just his eyes, which are the mirror of the soul, that reveal the horror that the spectator can't see. Is he afraid? Maybe, but he holds it in, and that's the incredible thing about him . . . That's what Cherniakovski was like . . . He held it in. Overall, he was a good guy, a down to earth guy . . . He was in exile for a while, I think . . . It was too bad he had to give up his poetry workshop, we had fun, but what else could he do? How long was I in the workshop? My whole youth, pal! And I got to know the Pons sisters, absolutely. Two pretty girls, good poetesses. Especially Edna Pons. I'm forgetting the other one's name. Lisa, that's right. Lisa and Edna Pons. Cherniakovski's pride and joy. Of the rest of the workshop, well, I remember two journalism kids, two or three other literature kids, the actor Javier Oyarzún, he struck it lucky, the bastard, and you, of course . . . What did you say your name was? Belano? The talker! Rules Boy Belano. Of course I remember. It might not seem like it, but I do. The speechmaker, right? Don't be embarrassed, Slim! Those were good times! Did I notice some stranger at the workshop before the coup? Exactly how long are we talking? Two or three months before? Man, strangers plural, in those days it was like a three-ring circus, there were all kinds of strangers, people who came in just to read a manifesto or to spend the afternoon: we were all fired up and partying twenty-four seven, don't you remember? And the workshop was always open . . . Not like Fernández's, which was stricter and more elitist. A poet? Slim, man, in those days we were all poets. Let me tell you something: Cherniakovski was the only one who seemed to know everyone, he's the one who could shed some light for you, but who knows where Cherniakovski is at this point in the game. That's all I can tell you, sorry. Rules Boy Belano! It's been a pleasure talking to you, man, but I have to go. Duty calls and I can still ring a few bells. It's hard to sell appliances door to door, but it's a steady job and with sales on the installment plan, all the better. Keep in mind that we're virtually the only business in the trade. I can't handle competition, Slim . . . No, let me get this . . . I have cash and One Eye here gives me a discount . . .

The Dream (2)

The kid in the white shirt walked the streets of the dark city . . . In the distance, silhouetted against the horizon, he saw the movie theater . . . But no, to say that it was silhouetted might erroneously suggest that it was on level ground, which was not the case . . . The streets rose and fell, stone staircases everywhere, gleaming in the night . . . The city, or at least this part of the city, seemed to be built on hills and crags . . . Uneven ground, paved with stone and cement, flanked by ravines filling up with black garbage bags as shiny as stones . . . And there were columns . . . Roman or Greek columns, holding urns . . . Urns plain and simple: the flowerpots of hell, muttered the boy . . . The kid glanced sidelong at the urns (flowerless) and the pillars . . . The kid was in a hurry, I know; it's not that he was scared . . . If I could climb a pillar, he thought, and reach into one of those pots . . . On the kid's face, hidden in shadows, a white smile with yellow streaks like strands of gold appeared . . . Imperceptibly, the silhouette of the movie theater loomed larger . . . There was no one in the stone and cardboard ticket booth . . . In any case, the kid had no plans to buy a ticket . . . He strode along the inner corridors of the movie theater . . . The corridors seemed like sections of an underground parking garage, they were too wide and the curtains that covered the cement wall barely concealed a swarm of pipes . . . Finally he pushed through double doors and stepped into a side gallery . . . From here he could see only part of the screen . . . The faces projected, a close-up of two platinum blondes, moved with exasperating slowness . . . Still standing, the kid watched the scene . . . The gallery was long and narrow . . . At the back were stacks of cane chairs and a row of seats rotted by the rain . . . The kid took a pack of Cabañas and a gold lighter out of his pocket . . . Along with the knife, they were his only possessions . . . He lit a cigarette and the smoke veiled his eyes like a tiny screen between him and the Diorama screen . . .

The Oarsman of Fate

Walt Whitman's daughters have hairy balls
Walt Whitman's daughters are gilded dolls
Walt Whitman's daughters sail as night falls
Eating breasts
Of turkey

> *Signed (in the air):*
> *Carlos Ramírez*
> *FACh Lieutenant*

What do you think of the poem?" asks Bibiano Macaduck.

"I don't know . . ."

"It's crap. The fucking goose-stepper thinks he's Céline."

"Are you including him in your *Signals*, too?"

"His complete works, compadre. The acme of the arrogance brigades, confound them, pack of morons . . ."

"But this poem isn't in the *Watchful Eye* . . ."

"Ah, but we have our sources. The poem in question turned

up at the Concepción Library on the shelf of lost works, between a monograph on the Seventh Regiment (an insane book that has our valiant troops scaling the slopes of Machu Picchu) and a Crawford and Sons volume on certain forays of Chile's premier botanist, full of sketches of the nation's flora and some of its fauna. What was the botanist's name, for Christ's sake? There must be something wrong with me, Rules Boy! I remember the publishing house, gone more than sixty years now, and I can't remember the botanist."

"Philippi."

"That's right. Rudolf Amand. God, what's wrong with me!"

"Relax, Macaduck. You found it between the Seventh Regiment and Philippi. But what did you find, exactly?"

"The journal with the poem in it, you dolt. Poems by Ramírez, some guy, Ismael Copero, and somebody else I can't remember. All of it crammed into an oversize eight-page booklet. The title of this monstrosity was *Semana Santa*, I shit you not. *Semana Santa*, get it? Initials: SS."

"Take it easy."

"Fine . . ."

"So where can I see this journal?"

"I told you, dumb ass, in the library. I'll make you a map so you can find the famous shelf without getting scrambled. Some strange books are buried in that dump. On Ramírez's shelf, you've got the Italian Fascists cuddling up to the Nazis and the National Unionists. Or their artistic manifestations. I mean: thugs on the plane of the sublime. The truth is, there's not much to choose between them, but you can trace the resolve. A straight line from the turn of the century, followed relentlessly, sometimes successfully and sometimes not: usually not. Occasionally I try to imagine what the rat who drops books off there must be like. The rat or the monk."

"I'll go and see it with my own eyes," I said.

"Better wait and read my *Signals*. Poking around in the dust will only confuse you more, Rules Boy."

"I'm going anyway," I said.

"What do you think he meant by saying that the daughters have hairy balls?"

"That they're men, obviously, Bibiano. Walt Whitman's daughters are men. Which is why they have hairy testicles . . . He must be referring to Neruda, Sandburg, de Rokha, Vachel Lindsay . . ."

"What about when he says that they're gilded dolls?"

"Man, 'dolls' is there to rhyme with 'balls,' that's the only reason I can think of. Unless the point is that they have money. Golden girls. But I doubt it."

"What about Walt Whitman's daughters sailing as night falls?"

"Same thing: it's for the rhyme. Makes no difference whether they sail as night falls or whether they sink their ships, like Hernán Cortés."

"Look, this is how I see it. Walt Whitman is America. 'Walt

Whitman's daughters have hairy balls' is a reference to the Amazons or the angels, the original inhabitants of the continent. The second line, about gilded dolls, means that the Amazons have forgotten their true nature and gotten mixed up with the new throngs of European immigrants, and on top of that they have gold: money or wisdom. The third line, when the daughters of Walt Whitman sail as night falls, is a reference to the Amazons' voyage to America. When you brought up Hernán Cortés, you unintentionally came close to hitting the nail on the head. The fourth and fifth lines, in which they eat turkey breasts, suggests—no, flat out states—that the Amazons came down to Earth devouring their parents, the gods of heaven. Devouring them with smiles on their faces, I'd say."

"You're messing with me, Macaduck."

"Actually, the events described in the poem aren't in chronological order. If we read it this way around, our birdie will sing a different tune: 'Walt Whitman's daughters sail as night falls / Eating breasts / Of turkey / The daughters of Walt Whitman have hairy balls / The daughters of Walt Whitman are gilded dolls,' and even better: insert the adverb 'today.' Today Walt Whitman's daughters (now, at this moment of struggle and destruction) are gilded dolls (they mingle complacently with decent working women, decent wives and mothers). And, as I'm sure you know, in some cultures the turkey is synonymous with sovereignty, wealth, and power . . . In America, and Europe too, the turkey stands for the father . . ."

"I always thought that kids who acted dumb were called turkeys. In school that's what they called me for a while."

"That's true, too, that's the flip side of it . . . We want to believe that the gods are stupid. But we don't lift a finger in the face of their wrath. Only the Amazons have ever been capable of eating them . . ."

"So, according to you, the hidden message of the poem is . . ."

"I'm not surprised you got a zero in mythology, Rules Boy. These chicks devour their parents and come down to earth thinking they're the shit, prancing around, even eating! Can you imagine the movie? Like the dinner party from *Venus Attack*, when an H-bomb is dropped on San Francisco and the guests come out on the terrace carrying chicken wings and glasses of wine, and they keep chewing and sipping as the mushroom cloud grows in the distance, have you seen it?"

"I saw it."

"Well, it's the same thing. The Amazons step out of their ships, victorious, feeling the peace that settles in the pores once the sweat has dried and everything is over. They come, they see, and they conquer. Still, the mere fact that a poet (especially when that poet is Carlos Ramírez) has testified to their arrival hides the seed or promise of destruction."

"Whose destruction?"

"Come on, man, the Amazons'."

"But why? Why would he destroy them?"

"I'll tell you, but don't yell. I could quote some sixty psychology books. But I'll make it brief: the guy has a problem with women . . ."

"Oh, that's all . . ."

"No, that's not all. He's got muscle—that's how I'd put it. The son of a bitch, if I can take poetic license, is an oarsman of fate . . ."

Cherniakovski Presents Two Images of India at the University of Concepción Poetry Workshop, 1972

The photographs come from two photographers, two books, and two ways of seeing India. Some are by Englishman Frederic Chester, from the book *The Wellspring of the Aryan Race*. The others, illustrations to *The Chaste Secrets*, by Dr. (Mrs.) Amalfitano, were taken by the Argentine photographer Eduardo "Lorito" Lozano. I think they complement each other, even if the complementing takes place in a savage realm, full of mirrors and heat. The faces, however, are noble and indifferent, as if they know something that we don't. As if they've come to accept something—perhaps after a millennial struggle—that we likely would not. Cherniakovski's face was contorted . . . I remember that it was winter and it was pouring rain. The Pons sisters, Javier Oyarzún, Fuenzalida, and I were all there, talking

Rilke. Cherniakovski arrived ten minutes late. He was carrying a slide projector. The projector was wet and so was he. Not bothering to dry himself off, he plugged in the projector and began to show the slides. There was no need to close the curtains: low black clouds covered the sky. Rain streaked the windows. That's a Brahmin, said Cherniakovski. Shot of a man with white hair and a white beard, dark skin, dark eyes, lips parted as if in conversation with the man on the other side of the lens. Cherniakovski sucked in air through his nose. Then came photographs of villages and cities, though it was hard to tell which was which. Boys in shorts, Talcahuano, said Javier Oyarzún. I searched for Cherniakovski's face in the semidarkness. His expression was stern and his eyes were glued to the screen. The Brahmin, whispered Cherniakovski. Again we saw the old man with the white beard, now sitting on a stone. Then a bright-red bus with white stripes, packed to the brim, and the statue of a god in a shrine by the side of the road. The god's eyes were green. The projector made a sound like an eggbeater and between slides the screen went blank: a weirdly illuminated stretch of wall. Some of us lit cigarettes. Cherniakovski said: that's a Brahmin, do you know what he's doing? His tone of voice made us shudder for some inexplicable reason. The rain seemed to fall inside the workshop. When we tried to look closer, the slide was gone. Encore, said Javier Oyarzún, but now other snapshots of the city's streets and inhabitants appeared. Indians eating in markets, old women with goods for sale on the ground, beggars in black Ray-Bans. Outside the rain literally lashed the walls. On the screen: a road, the old Brahmin, and the photographer's shadow. Then another photograph, closer up, the Brahmin casting a sideway glance at the lens with an apologetic smile. In the next one, the Brahmin's back was to the photographer and he was walking toward a city that could be glimpsed on the horizon. The city was barely visible and the air was dirty, stung with smoke and fog. There were five or six more slides until the old man disappeared around a bend. Cherniakovski coughed. What is the Brahmin doing? he asked. After some discussion, all we could say was that the Brahmin was walking toward a city. Calcutta? asked Javier Oyarzún. Bombay, said Cherniakovski. And the old man wasn't just walking, he was staring at the ground. Why? So he doesn't kill anything. Not even a single ant. Which is why the trip takes so long when he travels by foot—and these saints only travel by foot, I think, though I can't swear to it. A fifteen-mile walk can take four days, but they don't care. These people would rather die than hurt a butterfly. Now look at this. We sighed and turned our eyes to the screen again. We were definitely better off with Rilke. A room in India. Candles burning and faces emerging from the darkness as if from a black pool, smiling at the camera. Women? No, men wearing saris, their eyes made up. Transvestites, said Javier Oyarzún. Eunuchs, came Cherniakovski's voice from the rear of the workshop. I looked at him. His eyes stared, dazzled by the halo of light. The eunuchs were having a party. In a corner of the room, a boy. He's naked. A man with long white hair ties the boy's little testicles with a yellow ribbon. Cherniakovski let the white light linger on the wall. Now they go ahead and castrate him, he said. The operation is performed by the eunuchs' guru. We saw the skinny face of the boy. Ten, maybe eleven. Skinny and smiling. And Gabriela Mistral is dead, we heard Cherniakovski say in a soft, very dangerous voice. On this detail I must insist: his voice was as lethal as a razor-sharp boomerang, and so real that I ducked my head. Where the hell did you get these photographs? asked Javier Oyarzún, shrinking back in his seat, horrified. Cherniakovski didn't reply. He lit a cigarette and sat down in one of the many empty chairs. The projector kept running on its own. Its rattle gradually meshed with the sound of the rain. The rain seemed to say: get outside and enjoy your youth. Indians walking, working, eating, sleeping, but especially Indians walking. As if the slides were stuck . . . With my head on fire I took a last look at the screen. I seemed to see Juan Cherniakovski there, very dirty, his hair longer, smoking a cigarette and walking in the crowd. But probably it was just another Indian.

Bibiano Macaduck's Lecture
at the Cortapalos Club
of Concepción

When the war was over, Cherniakovski left the country. I guess he was looking for adventure or a break or he was trying to wipe the visions of delirium from his head. The fact is that he went to one of those Latin American cities that do their best to simulate hell. It had it all: gunmen, beggars, whores, child exploitation, everything you could ask for. Cherniakovski moved in with a reporter. In those days, of course, his name wasn't Cherniakovski. Let's say he went by Víctor Díaz. At first he lived a relatively quiet life. Maybe that was because he never went out. Víctor Díaz was a homebody. He got up late, past noon, brewed himself some coffee, and took his time drinking it. According to the reporter, Víctor Díaz wrote poems, short ones and not many of them, but all very polished, as was the norm among his old friends from Concepción. If you were born in the forties, you wrote short poems. If you were born in the fifties, you wrote epics. If you were born in the sixties, you wrote flatlined electroencephalograms. Ha ha, that's a joke. Anyway: Víctor Díaz went back to writing little poems and he left the reporter's house only to buy food and the like. Until one night he agreed to go out partying with some friends (the reporter's friends) and he was introduced to the red-light district. Bad news. His eyes, which had seemed to soften in the peace and quiet, grew sharp again. His whole body was on fire after that first night. The next week, he ventured out again, but this time alone. And every night after that. According to the reporter, Víctor Díaz was asking to be stabbed or shot, but you and I know how tough Cherniakovski was. The lucky bastard! End result: he took a prostitute as a lover. She was fifteen or sixteen, and she had a twelve-year-old brother. The pimps of the red-light district wanted to sell the kid. Whether as a rent boy or as fresh meat for organ transplants, it's not clear. Both were lucrative prospects. Víctor Díaz inhaled all the information he got from his lover like an addict going through withdrawal. There are men, I swear, who have some mysterious—even supernatural—ability to get their hands on any kind of weapon in any situation. Víctor Díaz was one of them. One night, he turned up with a Spanish Luger and he shot two pimps and three bodyguards. The sight of blood went to his head. Though according to other versions, he only killed one person. And I have a strong hunch of my own: the dead man was the prostitute's father (though not the little brother's). Either way, a crime was committed. There was blood. And it would all have turned into your typical tropical catastrophe were it not for the woman in this story. We can thank our lucky stars that the teenage prostitute had more sense and smarts than anyone could have imagined, because otherwise Víctor Díaz would be dead. Though we have our doubts about that. Anyway: the girl hid him, and we can guess that sooner or later they left the country. The prostitute, her little brother, and Víctor Díaz. The latter had contacts, and it seems that his companions came along for the ride. The three of them set off for some European country. Did Víctor Díaz marry his teen lover? Did the little brother go to school, did he make a place for himself in that strange and extraordinary culture? Did he learn to speak French, English, German? What was Víctor Díaz's victory, exactly? Was it finding them a home in a suburb of Development? We'll never be able to answer these questions with full confidence. Víctor Díaz got them settled, and after a while he left again. International terrorism was summoning our compatriot to other tasks . . .

Bibiano Macaduck's Lecture at the Cortapalos Club of Concepción (2)

I've spoken about a child and a sacrifice. *Sacrifice* in the commercial sense of the word. Now I think I should add a thing or two. Traffic in children's organs spread across Latin America at more or less the same time as Juan Cherniakovski (or Víctor Díaz) was wandering the Bolivarian stage with bloodshot eyes. And you're right, the image isn't mine—I stole it from some tabloid. The story, I think, unfolds like a performance at one of those so-called art house theaters: in the artificial dark of night, Víctor Díaz, one of legions of shuddering, sleepy Latin American macho men, arrives by chance at the heart of the slaughterhouse. The scenery is red and children roam a refrigerated corral awaiting their fate, which is to fly legally or clandestinely to private clinics in the United States or Canada—in some cases, clinics in Mexico, Guatemala, Puerto Rico—where they will undergo an operation. Everybody knows (since now and then *El Mercurio* makes it their business to inform us) that the waiting lists for those who need a kidney, a pancreas, or a heart can be long. So if you can pay for it (and in Real Democracies there is money), it's more comfortable—and above all, safer—to go under the knife at one of these private clinics. The network is run by professionals and it's efficient. There's always material. This is important if you're an engineer from San Francisco and you need a liver right away or the party's over. It's important if you're a good parent and you know that unless your six-year-old gets a heart transplant in two weeks, he'll die in your arms. Love—as everybody knows—moves mountains and spares no cost. Self-love or brotherly love. Need drives the market. And the market grows and fine-tunes itself. In the performance we were talking about, children wander bleak streets under palm trees. Other equally bloody stories unspool in the same place, but fate, which is like the devil and unites alpha and omega, led Víctor Díaz—who once upon a time wasn't Víctor Díaz and relished the poetry of Gabriela Mistral—to immerse himself in this particular horror. The scenery is red, and gang bosses and bands of lowlifes stroll under the palm trees. Hideous crones, like the witch from "Hansel and Gretel," play the part of health inspectors. Beggar children, homeless children, are the most common source of raw material. They're relatively easy to catch and their absence goes mostly unnoticed, but they have one drawback, energetically decried by the medical teams of various clinics: they aren't always healthy, their organs weak or ruined. The gang leaders deliberate in the land of Bolívar and San Martín, and after these parleys, commands fly across the theater at a speed achievable only by serious operators. Under the palm trees, when a sun of glossy paper—perfect imitation of a Siqueiros sun—sets over the saddest roofs on Earth, janissaries set out to steal children who've been better cared for. Speaking cinematographically, we move from Buñuel's *Los olvidados* to some random Joselito movie. These aren't middle-class children, obviously, but the children of workers. In fact, let's call them the children of working *mothers*, so that Víctor Díaz's eyes explode like neutron bombs. Seamstresses, shoe factory workers, waitresses, teachers, the occasional prostitute with a heart of gold. The business advances by leaps and bounds. In the land of palm trees and beyond, everyone has heard of it and it is occasionally discussed in hushed voices. Publicly, nobody will touch it or go near it. The criollo authorities respond in time-honored fashion by covering their ears. Like the three little monkeys, like Harman and Ising's cartoon version of the three little monkeys. Worse, if possible. The bosses are efficient and keep a low profile. The press lavishes well-informed citizens with details of the drug trade and the arms trade, which carry on like something in the foreground of a Flemish painting, while in the background a long line of children are carted off to the slaughterhouse. (For further information, I recommend Auden, the poem that begins: "About suffering they were never wrong, / The Old Masters: how well they understood / Its human position; how it takes place / While someone else is eating or opening a window or just walking dully along . . ." etcetera, etcetera, though I suppose you've never heard of Auden, like good Chileans.) The silence, as I was saying, is almost total. Every so often there's a bit of news, not in the papers or on television, but in magazines, like stories about flying saucers. We know it exists, but the reality is so awful that we'd rather pretend we don't. That's human progress. Assaults on a deserted street are awful at first, and break-ins are even worse, but we end up coming to terms with both. We've progressed from the perfect execution to the concentration camp and the atomic bomb. We seem to have stomachs of steel, but we're not ready to digest child-killing cannibalism, despite the counsel of Swift and Dupleix. We'll accept it eventually, but not yet. Meanwhile business prospers under the palm trees, and the Siqueiros sun rises and falls like a mad mandrill. The witches touch up their warts with French makeup. The child hunters play cards and fondle their privates like degenerate Narcissuses, fathers and brothers of us all. Víctor Díaz (a man who really preferred the love of men) falls in love with an adolescent prostitute and embraces the Terror. His formula is expressed as the curtain falls: if Paradise, in order to be Paradise, is fertile soil for a vast Hell, the duty of the Poet is to turn Paradise into Hell. Víctor Díaz and Jesus Christ set fire to the palm trees.

Regarding Events at Perpignan Station in the Early Morning Hours of December 13, 1988

Monsieur Benoît Hernández, forty-three, married and a native of Avignon, who on the dates of this deposition was in Perpignan for the purpose of performing his professional duties, has provided documents confirming that he is a wine sales representative for the house of Peyrade, in Marseille, with no criminal record.

On the night of December 12, M. Hernández dined with M. Patrick Monardes, with whom he planned to finalize the sale of one hundred and forty cases of Grand Reserve XXX from the Viticulture Cooperative of Port-Vendres. Attached is a statement from M. Monardes corroborating this fact. It is noted that the house of Peyrade has had business dealings with the Cooperative of Port-Vendres for the past five years. M. Hernández and M. Monardes dined at Restaurant Coelho, where

M. Monardes is a regular, known to the owner and employees. Attached are statements from M. Coelho; from the waiter who served M. Monardes and M. Hernández; and from the cook, who was twice visited by Monardes and Hernández (they stepped into the kitchen, in other words). The two men were delighted by the quality and originality of the food and also somewhat inebriated by the wine they had consumed.

When dinner was over, they proceeded to the Leather Clock, a fashionable dance club located in the center of our town. Here M. Monardes and M. Hernández remained until approximately five in the morning, though neither of the two is able to say exactly what time it was. Attached is a statement from Jean-Marc Rivette, waiter at the Leather Clock, who confirms that he served alcoholic beverages to M. Monardes, known to him before the date of this deposition, and to a male companion of M. Monardes's, in all likelihood M. Hernández. In his statement, Jean-Marc Rivette mentions that he saw Monardes and Hernández dancing on the main floor of the Leather Clock in the company of two women. Interrogated on this point, Monardes and Hernández deny having danced at all, which leads to the assumption that Rivette was mistaken or that Monardes and Hernández were dancing in such a state of intoxication that they are incapable of remembering it.

From the Leather Clock, M. Hernández and M. Monardes took a taxi to the latter's residence, having made the prudent choice not to drive M. Monardes's car, parked two blocks from the dance club. Ahmed Filali, the taxi driver, confirms that he picked up a fare at the Leather Clock, but he was reluctant to give a precise time, estimating that it was between four and five in the morning. Attached is his statement, and let it be noted that the aforementioned driver neglected to record the time and location of the fare request, as required . . .

Regarding Events at
Perpignan Station in the
Early Morning Hours of
December 13, 1988 (2)

After they were dropped off at M. Monardes's residence, M. Hernández paid the taxi driver and dismissed him. M. Monardes's wife and daughter didn't hear M. Monardes arrive. M. Monardes confirms that M. Hernández accompanied him to the elevator (M. Monardes lives in a third-floor apartment) and refused to come up, despite repeated entreaties. At seven a.m., M. Monardes's wife found her husband asleep in the guest room when she got up to make breakfast. M. Monardes, a man of rather intemperate nocturnal habits, often slept in the guest room when he came home under the influence.

After leaving M. Monardes safe and sound, M. Hernández decided to take a walk through town rather than catching a taxi back to his hotel. Here we should note that M. Hernández's hotel was less than one hundred yards from the station. It's no surprise, then, that Mr. Hernández's walk concluded in the general vicinity of the station.

At this point, M. Hernández's statement becomes less precise, full of gaps and question marks. As someone accustomed to drinking, M. Hernández knew that a night walk would help to clear his head, especially when little sleep was likely to be forthcoming. According to M. Hernández's schedule, he was supposed to leave Perpignan at eleven a.m., en route to Bordeaux, where he hoped to close another deal with local winemakers. As usual, he planned to make the trip in the same vehicle in which he had arrived in Perpignan, in other words, his own car. So far, so good.

What caused him to set foot in the station itself? M. Hernández hypothesizes that he wasn't tired yet and that the morning chill made a cup of hot coffee sound appealing. Thinking that the only place open so early would be the station restaurant, he turned in that direction.

The main entrances to the station were closed. But not the side entrances, one of which leads to the post office and other agencies, and one to the platforms. M. Hernández doesn't remember which he took, though it's possible to deduce that it was the one leading to the post office. M. Hernández remembers seeing two sacks of mail in the hallway, but no employees. The post office manager, André Lebel, confirms this. At that hour, the employees—Lebel himself and Pascal Lebrun—were busy sorting the mail in the back room and it's possible that an empty sack or two had been left in the hall. Sacks aside, all that can be said for certain is that no one saw or was seen by M. Hernández as he entered the station.

M. Hernández's walk along the platforms was brief. He went in search of the restaurant and discovered that it was closed. It was at this point, M. Hernández confessed, that he began to feel a growing sense of unease. Was it something in the restaurant or on the platforms that sparked his unease? Did M. Hernández fear being the only person in the station, perhaps, and therefore the likely victim of some assault or other aggression? When questioned about this, M. Hernández responded that it never occurred to him that he might be assaulted, much less that he might be the only person in the station. According to M. Hernández, everybody knows that stations are never completely empty. The greater likelihood, given the early hour and the cold, was that the employees were all hidden away in their respective cubicles. So what did trigger M. Hernández's stated unease? The only possible explanation is his discovery that the restaurant was closed.

Except that the restaurant wasn't closed. When he didn't see lights on inside, this was the conclusion that M. Hernández reached, but if he had pushed the door open he would have realized his error. (M. Hernández can't remember whether the door was open or closed or whether he tried to open it, and he admits that it's possible he assumed that the restaurant was closed just because the lights were off and there wasn't a soul sitting at the counter, behind the counter, or at the tables.)

At the moment in question, the restaurant manager, M. Jean-Marcel Vilar, was in the kitchen with the cleaning girl and one of the station's watchmen. None of them remembers hearing or seeing anything. The kitchen door was closed due to the morning cold, according to M. Vilar. The kitchen is a long, windowless room with two vents, isolated from the rest of the restaurant. And yet, if the light was on in the kitchen, which seems beyond dispute, M. Hernández would have seen it through the glass. (In his statement, M. Hernández says that he didn't see any lights on inside the restaurant.) The cleaning girl, Aline Darcy, eighteen, arrested twice for drug dealing and an addict herself, currently in recovery, has her own explanation for why M. Hernández didn't see light coming from the kitchen. According to her, they were working by candlelight, at the express request of M. Vilar, who was trying to save on electricity. Questioned about this, M. Vilar and the watchman emphatically denied the truth of this statement. In a side note to the main investigation, we note that two days after the date of the deposition, Aline Darcy exhibited contusions and bruises to her arms and back. The bruises weren't the result of clumsy needle punctures but rather seemed to be caused by pinches or blows . . .

From Lola Fontfreda
to Rigoberto Belano

I'm Catalan. I'm an atheist. I don't believe in ghosts. But yesterday Fernando came to me in a dream. He stood beside my bed and asked me to take care of the child. He asked me to forgive him for leaving me nothing. He asked me to forgive him for not loving me. No. He asked me to forgive him for loving me less than he loved books. But the child made up for all that, he said, because he loved him more than anything. Both of them: Didac and Eric. Actually, *the children* is what he said, which could have been a reference to all the children in the world, not just his own children. Then he got up and went into another room. I followed him. It was a hospital room. Fernando undressed and got into one of the beds. The other beds were empty, though the sheets were rumpled and in some cases shockingly dirty. I went to Fernando's bed and took his hand. We smiled at each other. I'm burning up, he said, feel my forehead, how high is my fever? One hundred and seven, I answered. I don't know why, since there was no way to take his temperature. You're so precise it's scary, he said, but now you should go. I thought he had mistaken me for the Swedish woman. When I went out, I started to cry. I think Fernando was crying too. From here a person can go back anywhere, he said, please don't come in. I went out and sat on a chair in the hall. There were no nurses or doctors or family members anywhere. Soon I heard Fernando screaming. His screams were terrible, followed by whistles, and I couldn't stand it but I didn't move. Fernando was screaming from the depths of his soul, sometimes piercingly and sometimes hoarsely, as if his throat was scorched. He seemed to be asking for water. He seemed to be calling cattle. He seemed to be whistling a song . . . Then I woke up. I was shaking and soaked in sweat. It took me a while to realize that I was crying too. Since I couldn't sleep anymore, I decided to write this. Now I think I should send it to you.

VINTAGE CLASSICS

Vintage Classics is home to some of the greatest writers and thinkers from around the world and across the ages. Bringing you not just the books you already know and love, but new additions to your library, these are works to capture imaginations, inspire new perspectives and excite curiosity.

Renowned for our iconic red spines and bold, collectable design, Vintage Classics is an adventurous, ever-evolving list. We breathe new life into classic books for modern readers, publishing to reflect the world today, because we believe that our times can best be understood in conversation with the past.

A Note on Our Sustainability Commitments

We create Vintage Classics red spine paperbacks with the environment in mind.

We have minimised the carbon impact of our books by using low-carbon FSC™-certified paper. Our covers use minimal, reduced-carbon finishes and we are working towards making all our books recyclable. All red spine editions are printed in the UK using 100% renewable energy.

For more information on our sustainability commitments, please visit greenpenguin.co.uk.

Discover more in **VINTAGE CLASSICS** red spine